ISLAND
SMILE

LINDSAY MARIE
MILLER

DON'T MISS THESE OTHER BOOKS BY
LINDSAY MARIE MILLER

The Girl in the Woods

Emerald Green

Honey Gold

Me & Mr. Jones

Mr. Jones & Me

Jungle Eyes

Coastal Spirit

Single

An Arrangement

An Accident

Mercy

AND LOOK FOR HER NEW NOVEL
Available in January 2018

Chapter 1

It was a warm summer night in the country when Elaine Rochester curled her knees into her swelling stomach and gasped. A hand went over the large bump, her fingers pressing into the soft fabric of her night gown. But then the cramping, tightening sensation worsened as she rose into an upright position by her husband on the bed.

Awakened by the noise, Henry sat up and whispered, "Elaine?"

Wincing from the discomfort, Elaine turned onto her side and pressed the edge of her face into the mattress. Heat flushed across every surface of her skin in strong flames.

"Elaine, what is it my darling?" He touched her shoulder delicately. "What's wrong?"

"The baby," she replied with a shallow breath. "The baby is coming."

"I'll call for the doctor." Henry ripped the sheet back and leapt down from the bed.

Elaine yelped in pain with the arrival of another contraction, stopping Henry in his tracks. "Go, Henry!" she demanded. "What are you waiting for? Call the doctor!"

Not wanting to abandon her, Henry stood there contemplating the consequences of leaving her alone and then scurried into the hallway. After making a frantic phone call to the doctor, Henry bolted downstairs and woke Martha, their most trusted house servant. She lifted the skirt of her night gown as Henry rushed her up the staircase, rattling off every immediate thought that came crashing into his mind.

When the doctor arrived, Henry kept at his heels, aimlessly tugging at his elbow. "Do you think she is in a great deal of pain?" Henry prodded and probed.

"Henry," the doctor sternly declared, turning back to him at the entrance of their bedroom. "She is about to give birth. Of course she is in pain." The doctor patted Henry's shoulder and then continued into the room with Martha.

"Yes, but—" Before Henry could finish, the door slammed in his face.

Taking a step back, Henry set his hands on his hips and exhaled. His light brown eyes raced across the floor as he turned around and began pacing it. Frantic and frustrated, Henry rubbed his palms together until they were slick with moisture, his heart pounding with every shrill cry of Elaine's voice. How ridiculous that he was not allowed to witness the birth of his own child. He was the father for goodness sake. It was absurd.

As the clock ticked on the wall, Henry took a seat in the long corridor, his brow brimming over with sweat. He lifted a shaky hand to swipe the smooth dark strands of fallen hair out of his face. But then Elaine screamed and Henry's head shot up at the agonizing sound. It was painful to listen to, and he imagined it must have been all the more painful to watch. Regardless, he wanted to be present and ease her current disposition in some fashion or form, even if her pain was the kind that could not be shared.

Henry took to pacing the floor again when Elaine cried out his name. His long fingers ran through his mane then over and across the stubble of his beard. Turning his head from side to side, Henry marched up and down the hallway until it sounded like he was stomping.

"Henry," Elaine crooned through the door. "I want Henry."

Desperate to draw near, Henry twisted the metal knob on the door and could hardly believe that it was unlocked. When he burst into the bedroom, Martha rushed forward with a stout palm in the air, blocking his entrance. "Mr. Rochester," she announced. "You aren't supposed to be in here."

"Henry," Elaine rasped. "Where is Henry?"

"I am here, my love." He turned to approach, but Martha stepped in the way.

"You are not allowed in here, Mr. Rochester," Martha reiterated. "Your presence is highly unacceptable."

"Henry," Elaine called again, her breathy voice shaky and distant.

"Let him in," the doctor ordered, impatient with the added distraction.

Though she did not agree, Martha stepped aside and allowed Henry to walk into the room. Once he brushed past her, Martha shut the door and all attention returned to Elaine.

"Henry," Elaine cried out, reaching her hand towards him.

"Yes, darling." Henry raced to her side, thankful that the doctor had overlooked his presence and willfully accepted it. "I'm here now." He knelt down on the floor beside Elaine and took her hand. "I'm here. I promise not to leave."

Elaine let out a breath of air as Henry gently kissed her forehead, glistening with beads of sweat. With another burst of pain, Elaine gasped and gritted her teeth. Henry thought the bones in his hand might break, but he dare not tell Elaine that she was squeezing too hard, that her grip had grown stronger, that she was hurting him. How could he complain when she was the one writhing in pain? If he must suffer too, then so be it.

For the next three hours, Elaine remained in a tortuous state of labor. Henry never left her side, but wondered if he had been selfish in causing her to carry and birth his child. Had he known the degree of pain she would be in, Henry might have considered the probability of procreation more somberly.

But her anguish and suffering were nature's price for the joyous infant she would soon bear. For months now, Elaine had shared her dreams with Henry. Dreams where they strolled through Central Park with a newborn child. A little girl. Sometimes two.

These dreams had visited Elaine nearly every night since their return to New York. Henry hoped they were a sign of all the good things to come, the exciting new life they would live together, the fulfillment of a promise he had made her long ago on the island. But now, watching Elaine give birth to their child, Henry knew that a dream could be defined by more than those images that delight or haunt one's sleep.

Life was a dream.

Elaine was a dream.

And the precious life Henry had created with her was one as well.

That hot summer night, at the first sound of his daughter's piercing scream, Henry truly believed that all he had ever hoped for or wanted were his two beautiful girls.

Taken aback, Henry rubbed his chin and gazed at the sight of Elaine holding their precious newborn daughter in her arms. Elaine glanced down at the sleeping child with tears in her eyes, delicately touching her thumb to the baby's cheek.

When she looked up at Henry, Elaine was pleased to find tears in his eyes as well.

"Would you like to hold her?" Elaine rubbed her lips together and smiled.

"Yes." Henry stepped forward, and Elaine gently placed the infant in the strength of his arms. As his eyes rushed over their bundle of joy, Elaine left her hand on Henry's arm. "What shall we call her?" he wondered, glancing back at Elaine.

Beaming with happiness, Elaine dried her eyes. "I thought of a name."

Henry cradled his daughter close to his chest, admiring her with fascination.

"You may not like it, Henry," Elaine feared, sitting upright in the bed.

"Won't you at least give me the chance to hear it?" he countered.

Elaine batted her long black lashes with a cat-like grin. "Lillian."

"Lillian," he echoed, letting the sound roll off his tongue.

"After my mother," Elaine continued. "Everyone always called her Lilly."

Henry watched their daughter as he replied, "Lilly it is then."

A silent tear slid down Elaine's cheek. She quickly wiped the moisture away and looked up at her husband holding her daughter in his arms. All those years she had spent stranded on the island alone with no one but Jade for comfort in the jungle, Elaine never could have imagined a life for herself. One where she had love and a home and a family.

Henry ambled towards the window, whispering sweet promises to Lilly all the while. As he placed the newborn child in her bassinet, moonlight shone through the nearest window. Henry closed the curtains to block out the evening glow, ready for the break of day even though it was the middle of the night. After planting a sweet kiss on his daughter's head, Henry returned to bed and slipped beneath the covers beside Elaine.

"How are you feeling, my love?" Henry lay down and combed his fingers through her black hair, hoping that whatever discomfort the pregnancy had caused would flee.

Without a word, Elaine stroked the edge of his jawline and smiled.

"What?" Henry cupped her cheek in his hand. "What is it?"

"I feel..." Her green eyes glistened with water in the night. "Happy."

With a crooked smile, Henry leaned closer and gifted a kiss on her lips.

"But something is wrong," Elaine said. "Something is not right, Henry."

"Darling," Henry whispered. "What on earth are you talking about?"

"The dreams. I have had dreams," she struggled with the words. "Dreams that I did not tell you about before. Dreams about you. Dreams about me. Dreams about the baby."

Henry dragged his knuckles across her cheek. "What sort of dreams?"

"Something is coming. Someone is coming. It is not good, Henry."

Henry took her face in his hands, unsure of what comfort he could provide. How could he convince her that they were finally safe? That they would never have to survive in the jungle again? That all that had happened there was over? That it had been over?

"They are dreams, Elaine," he insisted. "Dreams and nothing more."

"But what if they aren't dreams?" She touched his hand and looked deep into his eyes. "What if it is real? What if they are all real?"

Henry swallowed. "Elaine, you've just had a child. You need rest."

"I can see it in your eyes," she murmured. "You think I'm mad. Don't you?"

Startled by his wife's premonition, Henry gazed across the room at Lilly asleep in her bassinette. He had hoped that the pregnancy had been the sole source of Elaine's dreams. Since leaving the island, Henry had noticed moments when Elaine was not quite herself.

There was sadness, emptiness, loss. All present in her glowing green eyes.

Was it Jade? The jungle? The ocean? The life they once had together?

And then there was the matter of that package. The sand. The jar. The water and what had been floating inside. Like two pieces of evidence cut from the beast with a knife.

"Elaine." Henry swept his thumb across the length of her cheek. "I told you that I will take care of you. I will shelter you. I will protect you."

Elaine lowered her lashes in response. "Promise me something, Henry."

"Yes." Henry shook his head ever so slightly. "Of course."

Elaine met Henry's lively gaze, then flicked her eyes to the bassinette before settling on Henry again. "Promise me that if you have to choose between us, you will choose her."

Henry turned his face and took in the sight of their helpless child, only an hour old.

"Promise me, Henry." Elaine squeezed his hand and dug her nails into his palm.

"No, Elaine." Henry's brows came together in frustration. "I will make no such promise." He pulled his hand from her grasp and placed it on her shoulder.

Elaine fought through her tears and mumbled, "But you must."

"No. No!" Henry sat back and narrowed his eyes. "I will never give you up."

When her lower lip trembled, Elaine tossed her head back and cried. Never intending to upset her, Henry smoothed his hands along the side of her arms and brushed his mouth against hers. Then he trailed a line of gentle kisses from cheek to cheek.

Elaine curled her hands around the back of Henry's neck and clung to his warm body. As their torsos became flush, Henry cherished the tender embrace and rubbed her back. Her breath in his ear was a warm caress, reminding him of all that he had to lose.

"I love you, Henry," Elaine wept, resting her head in the crook of his neck.

Henry consoled her in the night, hoping more than believing that her emotions were no more than a natural reaction to giving birth. But as he held her body close, Henry sensed the fear flowing through her veins, because it was as palpable as a cool breeze in the wind.

Lying down with her head on his chest, Henry rubbed her arm and looked at the ceiling. Deep down, if he was completely honest with himself, Henry had felt it, too. Many months ago, when he had been foolish enough to let Elaine open that package.

"Listen to me, my love." Henry tilted his chin to glance down at her. "No one will ever take Lilly away from us." He watched her eyes, the way they glistened and gleamed.

Elaine placed her hand on his chest and counted on every word he said.

"And no one will ever take you away from me. Do you understand?"

Elaine offered a faint nod. "Yes, Henry. I understand."

"We are going to build a happy life here,

Elaine. Just as I promised you." Henry tucked a jet black lock behind her ear and tugged her chin up with his thumb. "We are meant to be together. It is the only thing that makes sense. And it is the only thing that matters."

Nodding once more, Elaine kept her head on his firm chest and snuggled closer. Henry wrapped his arms around her back and listened to the sound of her breathing until she succumbed to her own weariness and drifted off. As he stroked his fingers through her hair, Henry decided that no one would lay a hand on his daughter or his wife.

Unless they wanted to gaze into the open end of his pistol.

Chapter 2

O ne week passed and then two. With Elaine settling into the joys and obligations of a first time mother, Henry accepted an invitation for dinner at the Rochester Mansion. Since marrying and moving out to the country, Henry rarely found time for his mother and younger sister, Louisa. But he was thankful for the days with his father that the family business allowed. It was an ever-growing industry steepled in trade and commerce. One that Henry felt exceptionally proud and pleased to be a part of.

Upon arriving at the Rochester Mansion, Henry gazed out the carriage window and glanced up at the brick structure he had once called home. During his time on the island, Henry had accepted the fact that he might never see the place again. Now that they were back, he couldn't be sure what he had missed. The home he had made with Elaine in the country was the only place he hoped to spend the rest of his life.

Henry helped Elaine out of the carriage and led her to the front door, while she cradled Lilly in her arms, the sweet baby drifting off in a bundle of warm blankets. When Marge opened the door, Henry guided Elaine into the mansion and smiled. Not only was Marge the oldest member of the staff, she had lasted the longest, which meant she had more grit than the rest. Finding a servant to partake of Mrs. Rochester's unruly behavior was a task that not many could handle.

"Henry!" Louisa barreled down the staircase and leapt into her brother's arms, so filled with budding excitement at the ripe age of sixteen. Her blonde hair swayed as she ran, those long blonde curls tied back in a blue ribbon. She was especially ecstatic.

"Why my dear, sister." Henry set her down and held her at arm's length. "You sure are pleased to see us." He pinched her cheek and watched her bright eyes dart to Elaine.

"Hello Louisa," Elaine greeted, a healthy blush to her complexion.

Louisa stood silently in place, stopping and staring at the newborn child.

"Would you like to meet your niece?" Elaine could not help but grin, absorbing every bit of emotion flooding through Louisa's veins. It was a beautiful sort of fascination.

Louisa moved closer but remained hesitant, careful not to wake the baby. When she grew brave enough, Louisa reached out and touched the sleeve of Lilly's arm. A pleasant smile spread across her face, because Lilly had charmed her from the very start.

"She's so little," Louisa noted, inextricably captivated.

"She cries quite often as well," Henry added with a subtle whisper.

Louisa left her hand on Lilly's shoulder, unable to look away.

"Would you like to hold her?" Elaine wondered.

Louisa's blue eyes widened at the possibility. "May I?"

"Of course." Elaine cradled her daughter close as she gently placed her in Louisa's arms. With Lilly's head resting against her heart, Louisa could hardly contain the sense of pure love that had enveloped her. Deep down, she longed to become a mother one day and admired Elaine all the more for accomplishing the feat already.

Henry and Elaine shared an intimate look, acknowledging the way Louisa was so easily taken with their daughter. She was precious, the glue eternally binding Henry and Elaine to one another. Marriage was one thing. Love was another. But even with the two combined, nothing measured up to the delight of sharing a child.

"Oh, is that the baby?" Mrs. Rochester bustled into the room, worried that she had missed something. When she spotted her only grandchild pleasantly nestled in the arms of her only daughter, Mrs. Rochester held a hand to her mouth. A tear slid down her cheek as she welcomed the next branch on her family tree with limitless warmth.

"Henry, she's beautiful," Mrs. Rochester declared.

"Thank you, Mother." Henry gave her a kiss and hug, before she turned to Elaine and did the same. With the birth of Lilly, Mrs. Rochester's treatment of Elaine had turned from disgruntled to exemplary. Apparently, the addition of a grandchild worked wonders.

"She is beautiful, Elaine," Mrs. Rochester crooned, brimming over with newfound joy.

Elaine thanked her with a wide smile and then leaned into Henry's arm.

"Where is Father?" Henry put his hand along Elaine's waist, happy that the arrival of his firstborn was so well received. But he longed to witness his father's reaction.

"Hello, Henry." Mr. Rochester waltzed into the foyer and patted his son on the back. "Elaine," he acknowledged, offering a nod and hug. "What do we have here?"

Henry draped his arm across Elaine's shoulders as she settled into his embrace. "Your grandchild," he answered. "Lillian Carmichael Rochester."

"Look at her, Father," Louisa chimed. "Isn't she just beautiful?"

"Yes," Mr. Rochester admitted with a smile.

"Yes, she is."

As Lilly became acquainted with her grandparents, Elaine furrowed her brow in discomfort. Her eyes shot to the floor, though she was not staring at the surface beneath her feet. The dark thoughts were back, and they had returned stronger than ever before.

"Darling?" Henry smoothed his thumb along her cheek, perplexed by the look on her face. In the past week, her anxiety had lessened, but Henry recognized the slight line forming between her brows. She was afraid. Of what, he did not know.

Blinking rapidly, Elaine woke up from her daydream and looked into Henry's eyes. He threaded his long fingers through her black locks, offering what comfort he could.

"Are you all right, my love?" Henry cocked his head to the side.

"Yes." She moistened her lips and brushed the matter off. "I'm fine."

"Well." Mr. Rochester lingered in the foyer. "Shall we eat?"

"Yes!" Mrs. Rochester followed his lead as the two proceeded towards the dining room arm in arm. If not for Lilly in her arms, Louisa would have scurried after them.

"Would you like me to take the baby upstairs to rest?" Louisa asked.

"Yes, Louisa," Elaine muttered. "That will be fine."

Once she was up the staircase and out of sight,

Elaine turned back to Henry and clamped her hand around his arm. The blacks of her eyes were rapidly dilating.

"What is it?" Henry hissed, looking over his shoulder towards the dining room.

"Something is wrong, Henry." Elaine kept her voice low, assuming that anyone else in the mansion would mark her as mad if they overheard. "Something is not right."

"Elaine, whatever you are imagining, I can assure you that it is all in your head."

"No, Henry. Listen to me. Something is coming. Someone is coming."

"Henry!" Mrs. Rochester yelled from the dining room.

"Coming, Mother!" he called, turning back to Elaine. "Listen, darling." Henry cupped Elaine's cheeks in his large, strong hands. "You never spoke like this until the baby came. Perhaps that is what all of this is about."

Elaine tightened her grip on his arm. "You're not listening to me."

"The potatoes are getting cold!" Mrs. Rochester nagged with impatience.

"We'll be right there, Mother!" Henry yelled back down the hall.

When his attention returned to Elaine, the look on her face could have killed. "You don't believe me. Do you?" she inquired. "You think I'm simply imagining things."

"Elaine, I never said that," he defended,

clenching his jaw.

"You didn't have to." Elaine let go of his arm and climbed the staircase.

Henry watched her figure until she disappeared at the top of the steps. Frustrated and concerned, Henry stood there wondering how she could worry over something that was non-existent. Not only was the fear strange, it didn't even make sense.

"HENRY!"

"I'm coming!" Henry stormed down the hall and into the dining room, ready to devour whatever food he could get his hands on. As he took a seat, his eyes remained on the ceiling. He couldn't help but wonder what his wife and sister were discussing upstairs.

* * *

"Why Lilly?" Louisa wondered. "Where did the name come from?"

"It was my mother's," Elaine replied. "Lillian Carmichael. But she always went by Lilly. At least from what I can remember. I think of her often."

"Well, I think Lilly is a beautiful name." Louisa held out her pinkie for the baby to squeeze. Though her eyelids fluttered back and forth, Lilly was nearly awake, fighting sleep. When she opened her mouth and noticed Elaine, a bout of crying ensued.

"Oh, there now." Elaine swept the baby up in her arms and rubbed her back. "Is my sweet baby girl all right?" Holding her protectively close, Elaine lightly bounced the child until she fell back asleep. At the sight of peace on her face, Elaine placed Lilly in the crib Henry's father had specifically purchased for any time they might come by for a visit.

"Elaine, may I ask you something?" Louisa whispered, suddenly shy.

Undoubtedly curious, Elaine took a seat beside the crib and replied, "Of course." Then she took Louisa's hand in hers and gave it a reassuring pat. "We are sisters now."

"Yes," Louisa realized. "I suppose we are."

"Well..." Elaine motioned her hand in a circle. "Go on. Out with it."

"Someone else will be joining us for dinner tonight," Louisa revealed.

"Oh?" Elaine watched over Lilly for a moment. "Who?"

"Well." Louisa braided her fingers together and bit her lip. "I am in love."

"Love?" Elaine narrowed her eyes questioningly. "With whom?"

"A man named William." Louisa swooned and sighed, "William Pierce."

"William Pierce," Elaine repeated. "Who is that?"

"He is captain of a merchant ship," she boasted. "We met by accident a couple months ago. His carriage nearly crashed into mine, but mother blames our driver. We've kept the romance secret until now, and I didn't want to overwhelm you with it all."

"Do your mother and father know?"

"Why, yes! Of course," Louisa urged. "They were the first to know. And since William has already spoken with Father and received his permission—"

"What?" Elaine cut in, unsure how she felt about the news.

"Oh, Elaine. We are engaged!" Louisa jumped in place for a moment, hopping about the room like a frolicking bunny rabbit. "I have just been dying to tell you!"

"Engaged?" Elaine echoed, her pulse quickening with the word.

"Yes!" Louisa spun about the room. "Oh, isn't it wonderful?"

"Louisa, calm down," Elaine ordered. "Take a seat and listen to me."

Disappointed yet obedient, Louisa plopped down in the chair across from Elaine.

"How well can you possibly know this man?" she inquired. "What makes you so sure that this William Pierce is someone you can trust?"

"We've spent loads of time together. Just William and I. You will love him, Elaine."

Feeling queasy, Elaine grabbed Louisa's hand and said, "I just want to make sure that you are making the right decision for you. You are sixteen, Louisa. What is the rush?"

Louisa sat back in her chair and crossed her

arms over her chest. Her eyes were downcast, skirting across the floor, because she was wholly discouraged by Elaine's response. Looking up to her as a sister, Louisa had truly hoped for her approval.

"When I see the way Henry looks at you, I know that I want that for myself." Louisa lurched forward and wrapped her fingers around Elaine's arm. "I know everything is coming together rather quickly, but what does that matter when it is your true love?"

Elaine opened her mouth to speak, but Louisa kept on.

"He loves me, Elaine. He told me so himself. And I love him."

"Yes, but—"

"Oh, please," Louisa begged. "Please won't you be happy for me? For us?"

The doorbell rang as Elaine swallowed, her innermost feelings swelling with doom.

"Oh, he is here! How wonderful! Just as he said he would," Louisa cheered.

Before Elaine could speak another word, Louisa grabbed ahold of her wrist and dragged her into the hall and down the staircase. Mr. Rochester welcomed the evening guest with a friendly handshake, while Mrs. Rochester fawned all over him in the foyer.

"William!" Louisa sailed down the remaining steps and into his arms.

His back was turned to the banister, so Elaine

could hardly make out the sight of him, as the rest was blocked by Mr. and Mrs. Rochester. When Henry appeared from the dining room, Elaine joined him at the bottom of the staircase. "Who is this man?"

Elaine lowered her voice and replied, "I don't know."

"How I have missed you, my love," William cooed, gifting a sweet kiss on Elaine's forehead. He touched her cheeks with his hands as Henry gritted his teeth.

"Oh Henry, Elaine," Mr. Rochester called, his head popping up. "Come and meet William. He and your sister are engaged."

Henry and Elaine looked at one another before drawing near. As Mrs. Rochester stepped aside and looped her arm through her husband's, the esteemed merchant boat captain turned around for all in the room to see. His long blonde locks fell to his shoulders like a lion's mane, the rough, dark nature of his skin alluding to as much brutality.

"Hello there." He held out his hand politely. "My name is William Pierce."

Henry widened his eyes, while Elaine remained frozen in place like a block of ice. Neither could be sure if it were miracle or magic. Either way, the impossible was true.

Judas had returned from the dead.

Chapter 3

H enry," Mrs. Rochester prompted. "Aren't you going to say something?"

Henry balled one hand into a fist at his side, a slick sheen of sweat breaking out across his forehead. Judas gently lifted the corners of his mouth into a teasing smirk, his cobalt irises flaring like cataclysmic waves in an endless sea. "That is quite all right, Mrs. Rochester. Perhaps the young lad is shy when meeting new strangers."

"No, William," Louisa countered. "Henry, you are being rude."

Tackling the situation head on, Elaine extended a hand and stepped between Judas and Henry. "Hello, sir. I am delighted to make your acquaintance."

Judas pinned Elaine to the spot with an unsettling stare, delicately taking her palm in his. "Charmed, I am sure." He brought his mouth to the back of her hand and then gave her fingers a light squeeze. "What a lovely young wife you have," he waited a beat, then added, "Henry."

Flames rippled across the surface of Henry's skin. In that moment, he had never wanted to pounce on another human being and rip the man's jugular out with his bare hands so much. With the force and claws of that jungle cat Elaine had always kept by her side.

"Hello, Mr. Pierce is it?" Henry shook Judas's hand with a painful grip.

"Yes." Judas gasped and withdrew his hand from Henry's constricting hold. "Captain William Pierce, actually. I am in charge of the merchant ship, La Fleur Noire."

"Is that French I detect?" Mr. Rochester guessed.

"Yes," Judas nodded. "I speak it fluently. French, German, Italian."

"What does it mean, my love?" Louisa hung on his every word like a helpless fool.

"La Fleur Noire?" Judas checked and she nodded. "The black flower."

"How lovely and poetic," Louisa murmured, batting her eyes up at him.

"Well, dinner has been served. Let's continue this conversation in the dining room." Mr. Rochester steered his wife in that direction as Louisa and Judas followed suit. On the walk down the hall, the latter turned back and winked at Henry over his shoulder.

Once they were gone, Henry spun around to face Elaine. "Tell me I have gone mad. Or did you just see what I seem to have seen?" He held her gaze perceptively.

Elaine flicked her eyes to the empty hall and then grabbed Henry by the wrist, dragging him into the drawing room. With her heart pounding, Elaine shut the French doors and looked back to find Henry pacing the floor. Neither could understand why, at the exact moment William's true identity had been discovered, they had failed to utter a single word.

"How can that man be standing on his own two feet? Alive?" Henry pointed a long finger towards the front of the house, as furious as he was disturbed.

"I killed him." Elaine's worried green eyes dropped to the floor. "I thought I killed him."

"You did," Henry emphasized. "I saw his dead body with my own eyes."

"But I stabbed him in the chest," Elaine recalled. "More than once. I stabbed him in the heart. How could any man overcome something like that? He must be dead."

"What if it isn't him? What if we have both gone mad? Lost our minds?"

"No, Henry." Elaine placed her hands on his shoulders and gazed into his eyes. "It was real. All of it. Everything that happened on the island. I just can't comprehend how—"

"Maybe it's not him," Henry suggested. "Perhaps a brother, a twin?"

"A twin with the same scar on his cheek?"

"I didn't notice it," Henry confessed, narrowing his eyes in confusion.

"Perhaps you should look closer next time."

Henry exhaled aloud and moved away from Elaine, running his fingers through his hair. "If by some miracle, he did survive. If that truly is Judas in there talking to Mother and Father, engaged to my sister, then what are we going to do?"

"I don't know." Elaine thought the matter over. "But you can't tell them."

"What?" Henry hissed, jerking his chin at the sound of blindsiding his family.

"You cannot say a word," Elaine clarified. "To your mother, to your father, not even to Louisa." Her vibrant green eyes looked like liquid zeal in the light.

"Louisa is engaged to that man," Henry argued, raising his voice. "What on earth do you mean I cannot tell her? In no time at all, she could be his wife!"

"Henry," Elaine scolded. "Lower your voice."

"Elaine, I cannot bear the thought of that man in my parents' house!"

Elaine grabbed his chin and gritted her teeth. "Listen to me. You will not mention one word of this to anyone. Not to your parents and especially not to your sister."

"And why on earth would I do that, Elaine?" Henry growled back at her.

"Because right now, you and I are the only two who know the true identity of that man. Don't you see, Henry? We know his greatest secret. It's the only leverage we have."

Henry stepped away and let his arms dangle at his sides. Whether he would admit it or not, Elaine was right. To play chess with the pirate, they would undoubtedly need the upper hand. But with someone as ruthless as Judas, how long would the advantage last?

"So I am supposed to walk in there and dine with the man who murdered your father, who murdered Jade, who would have murdered you, with a smile on my face?"

Elaine touched his shirtsleeve. "You must act, Henry. Play your part."

Henry jerked his arm from her hold. "Fine. If I must." Fuming with rage at the position Judas had put them in, Henry opened the double doors and bolted out of the drawing room.

* * *

For the next hour, Henry held his tongue as Judas entertained the table with tales of heroic voyages at sea. Elaine took her fork and jostled the food back and forth on her plate, unable to meet his dark blue eyes. Every word that left Judas's mouth could not be mistaken for embellishment in her eyes. Elaine knew the difference between that and a lie.

"I plan to take some time off after Louisa and I are wed." He turned to the lovesick girl by his side and took hold of her hand. "We will honeymoon in Europe: London, Paris, Rome. It is my greatest intention to show her the world."

Louisa blushed until her cheeks were rosy pink. The touch of William's skin to her own filled her entire body with warmth. Of all the promises he had made her, a happy life with William Pierce was the one she looked forward to the most. Perhaps she was young and wholly inexperienced when it came to the intentions of handsome young men. But that was no matter to Louisa. For she was absolutely in love with him.

"I wonder, may I ask your age, sir?" Henry butted in. "How old are you?"

Judas smiled at either of Henry's parents, then turned his focus to Henry.

"Yes," Elaine reiterated. "I was just wondering the same thing myself."

Judas squirmed in his seat and let go of Louisa's hand. After planting his elbows against the tablecloth, he folded his fingers and eyed his glass of wine. "Well, if you must ask," he dragged the phrase out to no avail. "I am twenty-five."

"Really?" Henry set a finger to his lips. "You look much older than that."

"Well, I don't believe one's appearance should be an absolute indicator of age." Judas waved a hand at Elaine. "Take your young wife, for instance. From the look of her, I would assume that she could be no more than sixteen. Wouldn't you say so, Henry?"

Henry's nostrils flared as he made a fist on the

table.

"True," Elaine bluntly remarked. "But I am not sixteen."

Silence fell over the dining room table, as Mrs. Rochester racked her brain for a way to steer the conversation in a new direction. "And what of your wedding plans?" she said. "Won't the ceremony take place in a matter of weeks?"

"Yes." Louisa took William's hand and braided her fingers through his. When she looked into his beautiful blue eyes, she could see the wonderful future ahead of them. Like a breathtaking landscape they would paint together. She wanted to be his wife, his lover, mother to all of his children, no matter how many there might be. "Three long weeks."

Louisa admired her future husband with no shame, returning the cheerful smile that always seemed to be plastered on his face. To her, William Pierce was everything.

"Oh, there is so much joy in the family now," Mrs. Rochester boasted, more of an appreciation of loved ones than an excuse to brag. "First Henry and Elaine give us a beautiful baby girl, our first grandchild. And now Louisa will be wed within a month."

"Grandchild?" Judas echoed. "I was not aware of the new addition to the Rochester family." He lifted his wine glass to Henry and Elaine, though failed to follow through the proper notions of a toast. "Congratulations! I'll bet she is a beautiful baby girl."

As Judas took a sip of wine, Henry pushed his chair out from the table and rose to his feet, fleeing the room before he chose to do anything he might later regret. Marching through the house, he took the stairs two at a time and immediately proceeded into the room occupied by his daughter. Pulsing with rage, he reached the crib and gazed down at sweet Lilly. The sight of her sleeping soundly dissolved his anger at once.

"Forgive my husband," Elaine apologized, excusing his absence downstairs. "With the baby, neither of us have the luxury of a good night's rest anymore."

"Don't mind, Henry," Mr. Rochester said. "It is perfectly fine."

"Thank you." Elaine rose to her feet and held her hands behind her back. "But I would like to speak to my husband and check on our little one. If you'll excuse me."

As Elaine left the room, Judas spoke up in an attempt to delay her departure. "I would like to meet her," he announced, pleased at the sight of Elaine's frozen figure.

She swallowed and glanced back at him. "Who?"

With another sip of wine, Judas smiled. "Why, Elaine, your daughter, of course."

A grin smeared across his face, and it was a wicked one.

Vengeance surged through her veins as Elaine

turned on her heel and followed the path Henry had just taken. Climbing the staircase with a pounding head, Elaine rushed into the guest room and softly shut the door behind her. There she found Henry standing in front of the crib with Lilly protectively cradled in his strong, muscular arms.

"What is he playing at?" Elaine hissed, keeping her voice down.

"I do not know." Henry handed Lilly off to Elaine and headed for the door. "I must speak with Father. Alone in his study. I must warn him of the man his daughter is about to marry."

"No, Henry!" Elaine grabbed his elbow and pulled him back. The action stirred the baby awake as she started to cry. "Do not tell him who William is. You promised!"

"I won't tell him what we know." Henry straightened his coat. "But I am curious. What does Father think of this man? This William Pierce, as he calls himself."

"I wouldn't mind knowing myself." Elaine gently jostled Lilly in her arms as Henry left them alone in the room. When the door closed, Elaine sat down in a rocking chair and held the baby close. She could not bear the thought of Judas touching her child.

* * *

Frantic with nervous energy, Henry made a slow descent down the staircase and refrained from unleashing his temper. Thankful to discover that Mr. Rochester had already retired to his study for the evening, Henry rapped his knuckles against the door and sighed.

"Come in," Mr. Rochester gruffly called, perhaps sensing his son drawing near.

After searching the deserted hallway, Henry opened the door and stepped inside.

"Henry." Mr. Rochester balanced his reading glasses on the end of his nose. "Have a seat, son. And shut the door, why don't you?"

Obeying at once, Henry closed the door and ambled towards the vacant chair across from his father's desk. Once he took a seat, the matter of addressing his father became all the more taxing on his nerves. What could he say to him?

Mr. Rochester set his glasses down on his desk and sighed with sadness. "You know, Henry. When I look back on my life, I remember the birth of you and your sister. Now you have a child of your own, and Louisa has grown into a woman overnight."

"Father, Louisa is sixteen." Henry gripped the edge of his father's desk. "In a sense, that man could practically be her father. Does that not bother you?"

"What can I do about it?" Mr. Rochester questioned. "Louisa is no longer my little girl. She is a woman capable of making her own decisions. William is the man she has chosen."

Henry dragged his upper teeth across his bottom lip. "But Father, what if William is not the man for her?" He leaned in closer. "What if she is choosing wrong?"

Mr. Rochester squared his shoulders and pinned his eyebrows together. Reclining back, he rested his elbows along the arms of his chair and contemplated for a while. He was more curious than ever to learn the essence of Henry's thoughts.

"You disapprove of Mr. Pierce?" Mr. Rochester clipped. "Why?"

Henry braided his fingers together and then released them, flattening his palms side by side. "How much do we even know of the man? He is practically a stranger."

"Henry, tonight is not the first that your mother and I have been in the company of young William. You and Elaine have been occupied with the baby. But I can assure you that we have taken the time to know him. Do you really think I would give my blessing to just anyone? Do you really think I would give him permission to marry my daughter?" Mr. Rochester turned red in the face.

"Father, I have never mistaken you for a fool. Do not think that—"

"William is a good match for your sister. I do not mind the age difference, because he will be a better man to her. He will be able to take on the responsibilities of a husband."

"But Father—"

"Your sister has made her decision and so have I," Mr. Rochester barked. "You will not change my mind, and I doubt you have the capacity to change your sister's either."

Henry looked off, feeling as though he had been backed into a corner.

"I appreciate your concern for your sister, son." Mr. Rochester slipped his glasses back on and watched Henry through the rounded lenses. "But it is most uncalled for."

Hopelessly defeated, Henry accepted the outcome and rose to his feet.

"I expect to see you in the office first thing in the morning, Henry."

"Yes, sir." Henry left the room and closed the door behind him. After lingering in the hallway by himself, Henry heard the sound of Elaine's cry and bolted up the staircase.

Chapter 4

E laine gazed down upon her baby daughter, gently rocking her back and forth in the chair. In time, Lilly calmed to the soothing cadence of her mother's singing voice and drifted off. Relieved to watch her rest, Elaine held the child to her breast and closed her eyes with a taxing sigh. Henry may not admit it, but Elaine was frightened.

Failing to push the darkness away, Elaine stood up with a clouded mind and returned Lilly to her crib. Her pulse thrummed louder with every passing second, as Elaine recalled the dreams, the nightmares, the premonitions. Had she been a fool to ignore the imaginative warnings in her mind? For Judas was back. In true living color.

The door creaked open and Elaine listened, wondering why her visitor did not possess the decency to knock.

"What a charming room," Judas declared. "Do you visit your husband's parents often?"

Gazing down at her sleeping child, Elaine placed her hand on Lilly's chest. Then she lowered her lashes as red hot blood pounded in her eardrums.

"It is a lovely place." Judas took one step forward and then another, holding his hands behind his back. "The home you share with your husband is just as lovely, I imagine."

Elaine kept still with her back turned to him. She knew neither what to do nor say.

Judas grinned at her in silence. "Dear friend. After all this time, have you nothing to say to me?"

"Friend?" Elaine spun around and set her hands on the railing of Lilly's crib. "After everything you've done, how on earth could you possibly call me your friend?"

With a closed mouth, Judas quirked his lips to the side. "Your beauty has yet to fade," he noted. "In fact, I believe the child has only added to it."

Elaine shut her eyes and scowled. "What do you want, Judas? Why are you here?"

Judas hovered closer. "You have something of mine. I want it back."

Unpleasantly anxious, Elaine glowered up at him with a pair of glistening green eyes. "I stabbed you in the heart," she whispered. "I left you there to die. However did you make it off that island?"

Taking her remark as a compliment, Judas reached out and touched his palm to Elaine's cheek. She batted his arm away at the wrist and sneered at him in revulsion. "Such soft skin,"

Judas murmured.

Fuming with rage, Elaine got in his face and glared into his cobalt eyes. "You will never touch me again."

Judas moistened his lips and swallowed. "We shall see about that."

Elaine exhaled through her nostrils, and Judas's eyes flicked to her chest as it rose and fell. "I killed you," she rasped. "When we left the island, you were dead."

Turning to his side, Judas studied the intricate detailing on the bureau before him. "You're awfully wise," he said. "For a woman."

Elaine studied the angle of his jawline, the sharp, strong nature of its appearance. He gritted his teeth and smoldered, looking back at her. For a fleeting moment, Elaine recognized that Judas was beautiful. Evil, yet beautiful.

"How did you survive?" Elaine pressed, holding his predatory gaze without a blink.

"I assume you received my wedding gift." Judas crossed his arms over his chest and took a step too close.

Feeling threatened, Elaine turned her chin up, holding it high and mighty. Blood pulsed through her veins, as she had practically quit breathing. She never felt more uncomfortable than when he was standing in the room.

"There is an old legend from an ancient island tribe," Judas muttered, "that if you cut out the heart of a lion, you will capture its spirit."

Tears filled Elaine's eyes as she declared, "Jade was no lion."

"Perhaps not," Judas agreed. "But close enough."

"What do you want?" Elaine barked. "I have nothing of yours."

Aiming to increase her level of discomfort, Judas reached around her body and set his hand along the railing of the crib. Elaine stilled and swallowed, folding her arms across her chest. As she looked down, all she could feel was the stinging warmth of Judas's breath.

"The treasure is missing, and I know that you have it." Judas gazed down upon her, watching the paralyzing effect he had on her body. "You and your husband."

"I have no idea what you are talking about," Elaine coolly replied.

Wanting her full attention, Judas grabbed her chin until her eyes were on him. "I want that treasure, and I will have it, Elaine. Even if young Louisa must pay the price."

"You wouldn't touch her," Elaine remarked.

"She loves me, island girl." Judas stroked his calloused fingertips along her jawline. "And she will do whatever I ask her to."

"Leave my sister alone," Elaine demanded, though he had never been one to listen.

"She is not your sister," Judas proclaimed. "She is the sister of your husband."

Elaine turned her face away and clenched her

jaw. If not for the newborn child she was shielding behind her, Elaine would have fled the room in pursuit of Henry. Where was he when she needed him?

"Perhaps that is the problem," Judas said. "If Louisa were your own blood..." He stared at sleeping Lilly in the crib. "If she were your own child, perhaps you would behave differently."

Water blurred her eyes as Elaine uttered, "She is an innocent baby."

With the shake of his head, Judas popped the end of his tongue against his teeth. "She is human," he announced. "None of us are innocent."

Judas shoved Elaine out of the way and lunged for her child.

"NO!" Elaine cried, her voice amplifying into a mournful scream.

Henry burst through the door and looked about the room. After discovering the source of conflict, he ran and tackled Judas to the ground. The blade in his hand was now in Henry's, as the latter held it to Judas's throat.

"Do not ever touch my child or my wife again," Henry growled.

Judas curled his lips into a smile, as Elaine rested a hand over her stomach and cried.

"Tell me why I should not cut your throat, right now," Henry commanded.

"Because I wouldn't want to get any blood on that pretty wife of yours."

The remark set Henry off, as he slammed Judas's head into the ground. Having heard the scuffle downstairs, Mrs. Rochester barged into the room with Louisa and Mr. Rochester behind her. They froze in place at the sight of Judas pinned to the floor, petrified with shock.

"Good God, Henry!" Mrs. Rochester shrieked. "What is the matter with you?"

"William," Louisa cried, rushing over to him as Mr. Rochester jerked Henry up off the floor. "Oh, William. Are you hurt?" She looked at the love of her life with a pair of innocent blue eyes while her brother paced the floor and steamed like a bull.

"Yes, my love." William took her delicate face in his big hands and cooed.

"Son, you better have a very good explanation for this," Mr. Rochester declared.

Frantic with fear, Elaine's eyes met Henry's across the room as they exchanged like-minded thoughts without opening either of their mouths. With the scene they had just witnessed, Mr. and Mrs. Rochester would never believe that Elaine or Lilly had been in danger. If anything, Judas would be viewed as the victim and Henry the victimizer.

"It was nothing, sir." William curled his arm around Louisa's back, though it was hardly any trouble to bring her close. Her arms were already twisting around him like a vine.

Mr. Rochester set his hands on his hips and glared at Henry.

"I believe I have overstayed my welcome." William swept his blonde locks out of his face and left a brief kiss on Louisa's cheek. "Good night, my dear Louisa."

When William walked out of the room with a stride as smooth as that of a jungle cat, Louisa watched until the image of him was no more than a memory. "Henry, how could you?" She covered her mouth and wept, casting a resentful glower in her brother's direction.

"Louisa, you don't know what that man is capable of." Henry moved towards her with the intention of wrapping her in his embrace as a sign of comfort. "Stay away from him."

"Stay away from him?" She backed away from Henry and pain flitted across his face in return. "How dare you! How dare you ask me to stay away from the man I love!"

"Louisa!" Henry called after her.

But she sprinted from the room and ran down the staircase, chasing after William and calling out his name. She had spent a lifetime waiting for her true love to appear. Now that he had, nothing would stand in between the two of them. Not even flesh and blood.

Once Mrs. Rochester followed in her daughter's footsteps and shut the door behind them, Mr. Rochester stalked towards Henry and got in his face. "I understand that you do not approve of the man," Mr. Rochester reasoned. "But Henry, your behavior is unacceptable."

Henry held his tongue and brought his golden eyes to his father.

"I am disappointed in you, Henry." Mr. Rochester waved his fist in the air and took to shouting, the vein in his forehead loudly protruding outward. "How could you embarrass your mother and I in front of Louisa's betrothed? After the stunt you just pulled, that man may never step foot in this house again! Have you any compassion for your sister?"

Henry feathered his fingers through his hair and then reached out to grab Mr. Rochester's shoulders. "Father, if you only knew what that man has—"

"Henry, don't!" Elaine warned, her voice firm and desperate.

Mr. Rochester cast a glance in Elaine's direction, then pulled out of Henry's hold. For a moment, he stood their contemplating the matter, wondering if there was some important piece of the puzzle he was missing. But the young Mr. Pierce had won him over from the start, cordial and well-respected and kind. He would be a fool to let his daughter marry any other. So he stood by his original decision, no matter the opinion of Henry or his wife.

Rolling his sleeves up to the elbow, Mr. Rochester gazed at his son out of pity. "Your firstborn has taken a lot out of you, Henry. Why don't you take the day off tomorrow? Stay home with your wife. Spend time with your daughter. I am not asking you, Henry."

Stunned at whose side his father had chosen, Henry stood there gaping when Mr. Rochester walked out of the room and left him alone with Elaine. Rage boiled within him, because Judas had crept his way into the hearts of his father, mother, and young sister. What upset him the most was the fact that all three of them had chosen Judas over him.

They had believed the savage, the killer, the pirate.

But how could Henry blame them?

They didn't know any better.

"I'm sorry, Henry," Elaine whispered, feeling that she had done him an injustice.

Henry turned back to his wife and lowered his eyes. "We're going home."

Chapter 5

Henry roused awake at the break of day and sat up on the edge of the bed with his head in his hands. The cool white sheet pooled at his waist as he recollected the previous night. How had Judas ever managed to make it off that island? Alive?

His head clouded with worry and aggression, because the man must have been the devil. Who else would have the power to return in true living form? Henry knew that he should have believed Elaine weeks ago, for her nightmare had become his own.

Judas had successfully won over the affection of every Rochester in the household. Thankfully, Henry no longer resided under the same roof, carefully tucked away in the wilderness with his wife and daughter. But Captain William Pierce, as he called himself, even had Henry's father fooled. And now he was going to marry his poor sister, Louisa.

Fluttering her dark lashes, Elaine reached out and touched her hand to Henry's back. His bare skin felt increasingly warm, as if he were about to break into a sweat. Concerned, Elaine rose to her knees on the mattress and draped her arms over his chest, resting her chin on his shoulder. "What is it, Henry?" she whispered, kissing his cheek.

Henry clasped her wrists and tangled her fingers through his own. After staring at the ground for a very long time, he touched his lips to the back of her hand. With a loud sigh, Henry turned back to Elaine and looked into her exotic green eyes, so beautiful and pure.

"Henry," she gently crooned, rubbing her palm over the stubble on his face.

"Why do you suppose Father asked me to take the day off?" he wondered.

"After last night, I believe the answer is quite obvious." She shrugged apologetically.

"Yes, but Father knows me." Henry cradled her left hand in both of his, holding her gaze. "I am his son, Elaine. His only son. How can he trust that man over me?"

"He doesn't know any better, Henry." Elaine furrowed her brow at the odd position Judas had placed them both in. "If the roles were reversed, would you believe him?"

Henry looked at the headboard, contemplating the alternate reality.

"Do you understand how difficult it is to believe?" Elaine explained. "That a man we escaped in the jungle, a man who I killed, is back from the dead? Who would believe it?"

Henry dragged his lower lip between his teeth and groaned. "Especially now. Why wouldn't Father take Judas's word over mine?" He pressed the heel of his hand to his forehead. "I am a fool, Elaine," Henry confessed, resenting himself. "I played right into that man's hands. I did just what he wanted me to."

Sagging her shoulders, Elaine rubbed his arm and revealed, "I know why he has come back. I don't understand how, but I know why. He told me last night, Henry."

Curious fear flashed across the light brown of Henry's eyes.

"I know what he wants, and the price we will pay if he does not get it."

Blinking at the gravity of her words, Henry took Elaine's face in his hands. His thumbs brushed against the soft skin over her cheekbones. He wanted to touch her. Always.

Elaine glanced about the room, as if they could be overheard in the privacy of their own home. "The treasure," she hissed, placing her fingertips over Henry's chest.

He narrowed his eyes at her and flicked his tongue out to moisten his lips.

"He knows you took it. He knows we have it. He wants it back."

Henry nodded, accepting the circumstances laid out before them. "And you, Elaine? Do you believe we should return the treasure? Give it back to him flat out?"

"No." Elaine vigorously shook her head but kept her voice down. "If we give him exactly what he wants, then what will it be next? He will own us, Henry. Forever."

"Where does Louisa fit into all of this?" His mind was racing, as he had already figured as much. But he wanted to hear what Elaine thought. She knew more than she realized.

"He's using her against us," Elaine claimed. "The marriage is merely a threat."

"But she loves the man," Henry assumed. "Does she not?"

Elaine swallowed and stared into his eyes. "Profoundly."

Henry rose to his feet and stormed about the room as he got dressed. By the time he had slipped into a pair of trousers and pulled on a shirt, Henry jerked his shoes on and combed his fingers through his unruly hair. "I have had just about enough of this."

"Henry," Elaine cried, climbing out of bed in a thin nightgown.

Before she could react, Henry grabbed a pistol from the dresser and tucked it into the back of his pants. Then he pulled on his coat in a flash, cleverly concealing the weapon.

"What are you going to do?" Elaine approached him, her heart pounding.

Ignoring her question, Henry ambled towards

the bassinette by the window and leaned down to leave a delicate kiss on Lilly's forehead. When he stood upright, Henry met Elaine's tearful eyes with the clench of his jaw. "Elaine," he scolded with a huff.

"Don't go," she pleaded. "Henry, please don't go."

Henry cupped her cheek in his palm. "I won't have someone threatening the life of my wife and child. You mean too much to me, as does Lilly. I must go."

Elaine's sadness turned to anger, so she pushed him away. "And what if you get killed? Have you ever thought about that? You have a daughter now! Do you want her to grow up without a father? Do you want her to be like me?" Hot tears streamed down her face.

"I don't have a choice," Henry explained. "I never had a choice."

Elaine sobbed aloud, mourning all that had yet to happen, but most likely would.

"You asked me to choose her first," Henry reminded. "That is what I'm doing."

Elaine glimpsed Lilly breathing silently in her bassinette, then looked back to Henry.

"You don't know what that man is capable of," Elaine protested. "You know he killed my father. You know he killed Jade. But you were not there to watch. You didn't see it with your own eyes."

Henry turned a deaf ear to everything his wife had to say. Even though he had upset her, Henry knew that he was doing the right thing. There was too much honor in him to let Judas dominate the situation any longer. He kissed her forehead, but she failed to move.

Lowering his gaze, Henry stepped around Elaine and walked across the room. On his way to the door, he stopped at the sound of her pattering feet against the floor.

"Henry!" she cried out and chased after him, falling into his arms.

When Henry held her close, Elaine gazed into his golden eyes and crushed her lips to his. Her fingers traveled through his silky hair, as she whimpered at the warmth of his mouth. Henry curled his hand around the nape of her neck and fell prey to his wife's charms. It was one of the few weaknesses he had: her love.

Desperate to keep him, Elaine pecked her way down his neck and began unfastening the top buttons on his shirt. But Henry clamped his hand around her wrist and stopped her. "No, Elaine." He set her arms by her sides and gasped, "I must go."

Wrapping her arms around him with one final attempt, Elaine pressed her lips to his ear and whispered, "Come back to me."

Henry stroked her cheek and left her with a passionate, soul-stirring kiss. When he turned away and walked out of the room, Elaine wept at the sound of his boots against the staircase. At that very moment, Lilly awoke with a shrieking cry. It was not a good omen.

Chapter 6

I t was a well-known fact that Philip Rochester owned and operated one of the most lucrative clothing factories in all of New York. Aided by the hefty inheritance bequeathed to him upon the death of his British ancestors, Philip had turned a lump sum of money into an increasingly profitable business. With an Oxford education and wealth of start-up capital, Philip had every possible advantage pointing in his favor.

Thankful to have been blessed with a first-born son, Philip had every intention of turning full control of the factory over to Henry. But now that Louisa had discovered a fine young man to wed, Philip wondered at the idea of allowing William half. An equal stake in the business alongside his brother-in-law. That is, as soon as the merchant ship captain got the thrills of sea and adventure out of his system.

To atone for the damage Henry had done last night, Philip offered William a private tour of the factory at dawn. During the appointment, Philip planned to reveal his intentions for William and Louisa. Factory ownership would benefit both, as a more stable source of income that neither required nor called for such long trips away. If he was going to be a husband, William would need to maintain a more permanent presence in New York, especially when he and Louisa decided to start a family. His honor as Captain of La Fleur Noire was grand indeed, but would do no good when William had a pregnant wife.

"Well, sir." Philip led William into his office on the second floor. As the men sat down, Philip pointed through the windows against the wall overlooking the factory down below. "What do you think of my business?"

William leaned forward in his chair and rested his hands along his thighs. After looking over his shoulder, he turned back to Mr. Rochester with a smile. "Impeccable, sir."

Beaming at the compliment, Mr. Rochester opened a wooden box and revealed a collection of cigars. "Care for a smoke?"

"No thank you, sir." William waved the suggested away. "I do not smoke."

Taking one for himself, Mr. Rochester lit the cigar and took a lengthy puff.

"Why have you asked me here, sir?" William squirmed in his chair.

Mr. Rochester sucked on the cigar and exhaled, clouds of smoke drifting in the air. "After all that happened last night—and I do apologize for my son and his behavior."

"That is quite all right, sir." William smiled to show that the apology had been accepted.

"Well, I had planned to let Henry take over the factory when I retire." Mr. Rochester looked across the room at the window, admiring his surname on the glass. "But after last night, I wonder if Henry might need help. It might be wise if he is not running the business alone. Do you see where I am headed with this conversation?"

"Yes sir," William nodded. "I believe I do."

Mr. Rochester took another drag and then held his forefinger and thumb to his chin. "Once you and Louisa are wed, perhaps you would like to become a partner in the business alongside Henry. I have not spoken with him yet, but I plan to retire soon."

"Really?" William furrowed his brow, feeling of the pocket in his coat.

"Yes." Mr. Rochester took his glasses off and rubbed his eyes with his left hand. "Now that I have a grandchild, my priorities have changed. I am sure Henry and Elaine will have more children, and then Louisa will most likely be pregnant within the year."

"I see," William accepted. "So that is your proposition for me?"

"It won't be right away," Mr. Rochester explained. "But within the next six months, I would like an answer from you. Besides, once you are married, I imagine it would be difficult to spend so much time away from your wife. And then when you have children—"

"It is a perfectly good offer, Mr. Rochester. I thank you. Truly."

"Well..." Mr. Rochester reluctantly bit down on the end of his cigar. "I must speak with that son of mine first. But I just thought that I would give you some notice."

"I do appreciate that, sir." William stood up and extended his hand. "You are very kind."

Mr. Rochester shook his hand with a grin. "Nonsense. I am merely looking out for Louisa."

"Right you are, sir." William's smile ran from cheek to cheek, effortless.

"Would you like to see the rest of the factory?" Mr. Rochester glanced at his watch and then stubbed his cigar out in the ashtray on his desk. "We have nearly half an hour before the workers arrive."

"Sure." William rose to his feet with a laugh. "Why not?"

Mr. Rochester stood up and walked out of the room. "Follow me."

* * *

Leaning back in her chair, Elaine held a hand over her yawn and gazed out from her spot on the veranda. Lilly fluttered her long dark lashes in the cradle by the table, as Elaine kept a close eye on her sleepy daughter. Turning back to the food she had left untouched, Elaine dug her elbows into the table and sighed, worried for Henry.

"Mrs. Rochester," the butler announced. "Miss Rochester is here to see you."

"Thank you, Edward." Elaine rose with a smile as Louisa walked out onto the veranda.

As Edward left them in peace, Louisa forced a cherubic grin and greeted Elaine with affection. The two held hands and shared a kiss on the cheek before turning to the table.

"Louisa! What a lovely surprise," Elaine cheered to mask her inner fear. "Have you eaten yet? Join me for breakfast." As they each took a seat, Elaine insisted, "Please."

"Well. I suppose I could eat a bite," Louisa said. "Though I'm not very hungry."

"Did you already eat?" Elaine reiterated, wondering why she had not answered her before.

"No." Louisa folded her hands over the tablecloth and stared at them. "Mother does not know that I have left." She sat back in her chair when Elaine set a plate down in front of her. "Thank you." Louisa avoided eye contact as her complexion turned pale white.

"What brings you here so early in the morning, Louisa?" Elaine questioned. "Is something the matter?" She filled a biscuit with soft butter and strawberry jam.

Louisa bit her lip and studied the biscuit when Elaine put it on her plate.

Setting a silver knife aside, Elaine looked over

young Louisa's face and grasped her hand. "Louisa. Darling," she crooned. "What is it? You know you can tell me anything."

"Yes, I know." Louisa glanced up with a pair of shy blue eyes.

"Well then, what is it?" Elaine turned Louisa's chin up with her finger.

"It's William," Louisa blurted out, darting her eyes about in case anyone had heard.

Elaine dropped her hand from Louisa's face and sank into the back of her chair.

"Something, something is..." Louisa stumbled over her words, fighting for breath. "I fear that there is something gravely the matter with him. But I can't put my finger on it."

"Has he done anything to harm you?" Elaine probed. "Said anything to upset you?"

"No, no. Nothing like that." Louisa leaned across the table and lowered her voice. "But sometimes I wonder if he is another person entirely."

Elaine held her breath and kept her eyes on Louisa as she confessed.

"Sometimes, I wonder if I even know him at all." Louisa pressed her lips together.

"What do you mean?" Elaine asked. "What would make you say that?"

"William can be so secretive and strange," Louisa admitted.

Elaine placed her palms over each forearm and listened.

"Just this morning," Louisa murmured, "he came to the house and left for work with Father. But William wouldn't even speak to me. It was like he didn't see me at all."

"Louisa." Elaine grabbed her arm and squeezed. "When did they leave?"

"About an hour ago." Louisa lifted an eyebrow. "Why?"

Following her instincts, Elaine rose to her feet in haste. "Stay here."

"Where are you going?" Louisa wondered. "You can't possibly—"

"Watch Lilly," Elaine commanded, leaving a kiss on her daughter's cheek. "Don't let her out of your sight." She picked Lilly up, approached Louisa, and placed the child in her arms. "And whatever you do, do not leave this house. Do you understand me?"

"Yes, but Elaine. Why?" She stood with Lilly in her arms. "What is the matter?"

"It's William," Elaine confirmed. "He is not the man you think he is."

The skirting of her dress billowed across the floor as Elaine entered the house. Confused by fear, Louisa gazed out at the lush gardens and wondered if she had made a mistake. Perhaps she should have kept her worries to herself. But it was too late, as Louisa rocked the baby back and forth in her arms, for her precious niece let out a piercing cry.

* * *

Henry crept up the back steps to his father's factory with the pistol securely tucked beneath the grip of his belt. While he had no intention of using the weapon, he had never possessed an ounce of trust for Judas. Now that he had returned to New York under false pretenses and threatened to marry his sixteen-year-old sister, Henry refused to walk about the city without a means of protection.

Desperate to speak with his Father in private, Henry let himself into the factory and took careful footsteps between the assembly line of tables and machines. Even though he had foregone his father's wishes by coming to work today, Henry could not conceal the truth any longer. No matter what Elaine said, his father must know who William really was.

When he reached the length of the room, Henry climbed the staircase to the main office. After opening the door, Henry stepped inside and called out, "Father!"

The office was vacant, but Henry spotted the desk and found a steaming cigar.

"Father!" Henry scanned the room, then proceeded back down the staircase with caution. "Father!" he repeated, hurrying his steps with the pounding rhythm of his heart.

Henry circled the great big room again and then looked up at the windows of his father's office. Deep within the pit of his soul, Henry knew that something was terribly wrong.

In an effort to steady his breathing, Henry smoothed the sweat gathering in his palms against the fabric of his pants. Father must be here. Father is always here, he thought to himself. Why isn't he then? an inner voice answered back.

"I don't know," Henry whispered aloud, fearful that he had lost his mind.

Frantically looking about the place, Henry rushed to the back of the building, for there was only one area he had yet to look. The room where his father kept the safe.

Henry arrived in the dark corridor and reached the door at the end of the hall. White smoke billowed out from the narrow opening at the bottom of the door. "FATHER!"

Horrified, Henry twisted the metal handle but it wouldn't budge. Taking several steps back, Henry ran and slammed the weight of his body into the wooden door. But after three failed attempts, Henry pulled the pistol from his back and shot the lock on the door.

With the heel of his boot, Henry kicked his way inside and pushed through the smog until he found Mr. Rochester on the floor with a bloody wound across his forehead. Fire blazed about the room, searing and scorching everything in its path.

"Father!" Henry coughed, crawling on his hands and knees to reach him. "Father!"

Mr. Rochester's glasses hung on the end of his nose, one of the lenses cracked.

"Henry." Mr. Rochester grabbed his son's

shoulder. "I'm sorry for what I said."

"Father, what happened?" Henry pulled Mr. Rochester up, propping his back against the wall. "I must get you out of here at once. How will we put the fire out?"

"Forget about the fire, Henry." Mr. Rochester opened his jacket and exposed the warm red blood soaking through his white shirt.

"Father," Henry gasped, his eyes widening in fear and alarm. "We must get you to a doctor at once." Crouching down, Henry took his father's arm and curled it around his shoulders, struggling to get Mr. Rochester to his feet.

"Put me down, Henry," Mr. Rochester protested, coughing up blood.

Henry obeyed at once, flicking his eyes at the sound of shattering glass.

"Listen to me," Mr. Rochester rasped.

Henry's golden eyes darted to his father, ready and willing to listen.

"When I came to the factory this morning, I did not come alone." Mr. Rochester covered his mouth with a painful cough, as Henry helped him to sit upright. "William came with me. He broke into the safe, Henry. He has taken everything."

Henry swallowed and looked through the blazing flames at the Victorian painting of Queen Elizabeth I on the floor, as well as the opened safe it used to guard. A large portion of the treasure had been stowed away in that very safe. But now it was gone.

"You were right to warn me, Henry. And I am sorry," Mr. Rochester confessed.

"Father, it is not your fault," Henry cried. "The fault is mine."

Mr. Rochester gasped and winced in pain. "He is not who I thought he was."

"Father, I must get you out of here. You must see a doctor at once."

"No," Mr. Rochester weakly replied. "Don't move my body. Not yet."

"Father," Henry wept, heavy tears streaming down from his eyes.

"Take care of your mother, Louisa, Elaine, and my granddaughter. You must be the man now." Mr. Rochester looked off, his spirit fading away with each passing second.

"Father," Henry shook his shoulders and cried. "FATHER!"

"He told me his real name," Mr. Rochester mumbled. "Judas."

"Father, you must go with me now! You must see a doctor!"

Mr. Rochester drew a heaving breath. "He's going back to the island," he whispered. "And he is taking Louisa with him. Promise me you won't let him. Promise me."

Henry felt the pressure in his hand as Mr. Rochester squeezed it.

"I promise, Father," he wept. "I promise."

"Don't let him win." Mr. Rochester breathed and his head eased to the side.

"FATHER!" Henry buried his face in his hands and mourned, rising to his feet at the sight of his father's dead body. In a state of shock and outrage, Henry turned a table over in the room and slung the Victorian painting against the wall.

If he dragged his father's body out into the street, surely every onlooker would pin the murder on him. After all, Judas was nowhere in sight, and Henry had a loaded pistol in his possession. Plus, the violent scene Henry had demonstrated last night at the Rochester Mansion only proved a case against him further.

And then there was the matter of Louisa. And Henry had promised him. He had promised their father that he would not let that savage do anything to his sister.

"I'm sorry, Father." Henry bowed his head out of respect. "I'm sorry."

With a heavy heart, Henry fled the room and refused to look back. The fire had already spread down the corridor and into open territory, roasting every piece of machinery and equipment in its path. For the shortest of moments, Henry stood there and watched his father's business burn to the ground. When the fire reached the office, the window bearing the Rochester name exploded into shards of tiny, fragmented glass.

Henry dried his tears and walked through the flames with a pistol in his hand.

Chapter 7

By the time Elaine arrived at the factory, a crowd of workers and local townsmen had gathered around the place. Elaine yelled for her driver to pull over and stepped out of the carriage. When her shoes hit the pavement, Elaine held her head back and gaped in shock.

Bursting into tears, Elaine crumpled to the ground at the realization that Judas had burned Henry and his father alive. She screamed and cried, reaching for her husband. But he was not there. He would never be there again. Lilly would live a life without him.

"NOOOOOO!!!!" Elaine wailed, falling to pieces on the concrete.

The driver leapt down from the carriage and picked her up off the ground. When he removed his hat and bowed his head in sorrow, Elaine lost her footing and nearly fell over. Catching her arm, the driver held her body upright, as she failed to keep her balance.

"No, no, no..." Elaine whimpered, burying her face in the driver's shirt.

He threaded his fingers through the gray hair on his head, not knowing what to do. "I'm sorry, miss." Holding her in his arms, he continued, "I am so sorry, Mrs. Rochester."

When the fire department reached the factory, it was no use. So Elaine sat down on the sidewalk and studied the cracks in the ground, not caring if she ever stood up again. Time passed, maybe minutes, maybe hours before Elaine heard the voice of another.

"Excuse me, ma'am." The head of the fire department extended his hand and introduced himself. "We have found a body. Would you mind taking a look?"

Elaine took his hand and kept her eyes down as he led her away from the crowd. Behind the fire truck, the thin body of a man lay out on a stretcher, concealed beneath the covering of a bare white sheet. Cringing at the sight, Elaine kept the vision contained within the corner of her eye, prolonging the inevitable.

The fire department head pulled the sheet down to the chest of the body, careful to only reveal the face of the deceased. "Do you know this man?" he asked.

Tears sprung to Elaine's eyes as she sobbed aloud. "Yes."

"Can you identify him for us, ma'am? Can you give us a name?"

"Philip Rochester," she wept. "He is my husband's father."

The man handed Elaine his handkerchief. "I'm sorry, ma'am."

Paralyzed by the reality of Philip's death, Elaine stood there for what felt like a lifetime, just gazing out at the horizon. To say that she were merely in a state of shock would have been an understatement, for Elaine was traumatized, horrified, and inexplicably confused.

When she mustered the strength to take her driver's hand, he led her to the carriage, where she took a seat and stared blankly ahead. There were no words, no thoughts, no sounds, for all the darkness she had feared and anticipated had undoubtedly revealed itself. As the carriage rolled forward, Elaine maintained a weak posture, her body jostling with the force of the horses leading them. In an instant, she felt sure she would be sick.

Cold sweat collected at the nape of her neck and within the depth of her palms. Elaine looked out the window once they arrived at the Rochester Mansion, feeling like a ghost once she stepped onto the hard pavement.

Elaine knocked on the front door and then held her hands behind her back. Philip was dead. Henry's father was dead. Mr. Rochester was dead. But where was Judas? And where was Henry?

Marge opened the door with a smile on her face, pleased to see Elaine again. But then she pinned her gray eyebrows together and stepped back for Elaine to enter the mansion. Mrs. Rochester hurried down the staircase with the hope of visiting with family.

"Elaine!" she grabbed Elaine's wrists and kissed either of her cheeks. "How good of you to come after what happened last night. Have you brought the little one?"

"No ma'am." Elaine hung her head and avoided all eye contact.

"Well, Elaine. What is the matter? Why are you so glum?"

Elaine swallowed and moistened her lips, looking up and finding fear in the eyes of her mother-in-law. "There was a fire today at the factory," she confessed. "The place nearly burned to the ground."

Mrs. Rochester clung to the wooden post at the bottom of the staircase. Her hand went over her stomach as she grew weak in the knees. "Where is Philip? Where is my Philip?"

Elaine's lower lip quivered as she shook her head. "I'm sorry."

Refusing to break down, Mrs. Rochester held her chin high and slowly walked back up the staircase. Elaine cocked her head to the side as she watched her languid ascent. When she reached the top of the stairs, Mrs. Rochester went to her bedroom and shut the door. Taking a deep breath, Elaine looked about the place and took a seat in the drawing room.

When Louisa arrived, Elaine opened the door to find the young girl crying on the front steps. As tears streamed down her face, Elaine pulled Louisa over the threshold and held her close. "I am sorry, sister," Elaine whispered. "I am so very sorry."

Marge shut the front door and brought the pair of women muffins and tea. Neither touched the food or drink, too overcome with sadness to feel hunger and thirst. Instead, Elaine and Louisa sat across from one another in the drawing room, staring at the carpet.

"When William left with Father this morning," Louisa eventually said. Her eyes met Elaine's, as thoughts skittered here and there in her mind. "What happened?"

Elaine chewed at the inside of her cheek and inhaled. "I don't know."

"What do you believe happened?" Louisa fired back, wanting an answer.

Elaine opened her mouth to reveal what she really thought, while Louisa hung on to the possibility of every word. But then Elaine bit her tongue at the last. "I don't know."

Plagued with worry, Elaine rose to her feet and paced the floor, resting her palms at the small of her back. She walked over to the window and pulled the curtain back to stare through the glass. The sun would be setting soon, and possibly all of her hopes and dreams along with it.

"You do know." Louisa shot up and pointed

her finger. "Tell me!"

Elaine looked back over her shoulder at Louisa. "I was not there. How could you possibly expect me to know?" Then she turned back to the window and looked out.

"But you have some idea of what might have happened," Louisa presumed.

Elaine stared out at the ocean without blinking, her eyes glazing over.

"Don't you?" Louisa sobbed, her voice shaky. "Don't you?" she yelled.

"Louisa!" Elaine scolded. "Do you want to upset your mother anymore?" She pointed to the ceiling as Louisa's blue eyes drifted to the white paint above them.

"I am going to find him," Louisa decided. "I am going to find William. He will tell me what happened." She rushed out of the drawing room, headed for the front door.

"Louisa!" Elaine called after her. "Don't! You're making a rash decision."

"I cannot help it," she barked back. "I love him... and I hate him."

"Louisa, do not walk out that door!" Elaine commanded. Ambling closer, she clasped Louisa's arm and placed her hand on her shoulder. "Please, for your mother's sake."

Clenching her jaw, Louisa gazed up the staircase and then let her eyes drift back to the front door. "Let go," she sternly declared. "Let go of my arm!"

Accepting the inevitable, Elaine released her and took a step back. Louisa twisted the doorknob and rushed out into the open air, on the hunt for the man she loved, the man who had killed her father. She never imagined they would be one in the same.

Elaine walked outside and watched Louisa go. Then she crossed her arms over her chest and sat down on the front door steps. When her young sister-in-law disappeared from sight, Elaine threaded her fingers through her hair, hung her head and cried.

Chapter 8

Darkness fell over the city that warm summer night. Elaine trudged through the household listening to the dull beat of the grandfather clock in the hall. Her finger wrapped around a lock of hair, as she paced to and fro, waiting for Louisa to return.

At the sound of an approaching carriage, Elaine peered out the window. But the horses plodded forward, steering the unknown carriage farther into the city. With her blood pulsing, Elaine traced the nail of her thumb over her lower lip. For the past three hours, she had been panting and sweating, desperate to know the answers to the questions circling her mind. Where was Judas? Where was Louisa? Where was Henry?

A loud crash sounded overhead, as Elaine froze in her tracks. She took one step forward and then the next, hesitantly reaching the bottom of the staircase. Once she mustered the courage to take hold of her skirt and climb those steps to the top, the beat of her heart pounded loudly in her eardrums, like an approaching train on the track.

Uncomfortable in the silence, Elaine forced a lump down her throat and stared at the closed door to the master bedroom straight ahead. Her hands were shaking by the time she reached the end of the hall, but she pushed onward. "Are you all right in there?"

When there was no reply, Elaine gently rapped her knuckles against the door and called out to her mother-in-law. But Mrs. Rochester said nothing in return, further heightening the fear racing and coursing through Elaine's veins.

Surprised to find the door unlocked, Elaine twisted the handle and crept inside. Before she could enter the room, Elaine caught a glimpse of Mrs. Rochester through the crack in the door. Elaine shrieked aloud and crumpled to the ground in the bedroom.

Mrs. Rochester sat on the floor with her back to the wall, empty bottles of brandy all around her. Stifling her sobs with a hand over her mouth, Elaine looked up at the pale corpse of Henry's mother. Her mouth hung ajar with her head tilted to the side, her eyes glazed over and looking straight ahead, as if she were mesmerized by her husband's ghost.

Quivering with remorse, Elaine leaned forward and closed Mrs. Rochester's eyes. Then she sat back on her elbows and studied the deathly pale figure of her mother-in-law. As Elaine lay down on the floor, the side of her face dug into the skin of her forearm. Her glistening green eyes looked over Mrs. Rochester, sensing the sadness and misery that must have invaded her spirit moments before she chose to take the last drink, the one that would end things for good.

By the time Elaine rose to her feet, her mouth had gone dry and her limbs had turned to mush. With a handful of long, shaky strides, Elaine walked around the master bedroom and opened the jewelry box on the bureau. Mrs. Rochester's jewelry was precious and beautiful, a collection of gifts from Henry's father throughout their marriage.

Elaine shut the box with force and lifted her head to gaze at her reflection in the mirror. She blinked three times and watched a lonely tear streak its way down her cheek. After the fateful events of the morning and night, the Rochester Mansion would never be the same.

Exhausted and shaken, Elaine ruffled her fingers through her long dark mane and closed the door to the master bedroom behind her. Then she slowly ambled down the hallway, reaching her hand out to touch the wall to keep herself from falling down. Once Elaine reached the banister, one foot managed to move in front of the other, though she did not contribute much to the task.

Feeling like a ghost, Elaine walked out the front door and never even bothered to shut it back. She trudged out into the evening as the moonlight cast shadows across her face. With her arms limply hanging at her sides, Elaine stepped onto the sidewalk and continued alongside the road, her eyes skittering across the edge of black pavement.

When a mysterious carriage approached, Elaine numbed at the sound of horseshoes against the concrete. Not wanting to alert whoever may be inside, Elaine kept one foot in front of the other, as if the carriage were of no importance to her. But then the carriage stopped by the sidewalk, the door flipped open, and the passenger pulled her inside.

"Ah!" Elaine cried out, but a large hand covered her mouth as the carriage took off into the night. Fighting the firm grip around her body, Elaine tried to jump out the door, but her captor pulled it closed. So she bucked and squirmed, elbowing the stranger in the ribs.

"Ow! Elaine. Quit it!" Henry gasped at the bruising pain and let her go.

Turning around in the seat, Elaine deflated with relief at the sight of her husband. "Oh, Henry." She leapt into his arms and placed her head on his chest, hugging him close.

Understanding her reaction, Henry stroked his fingers through her hair and sighed. "Forgive me, my love," he softly crooned. "I didn't mean to frighten you."

"Henry," Elaine called, gazing up at him in the night. "Your father."

"I know." Henry swept his thumb against her cheek. "He is gone."

Elaine clamped her wrist around his forearm, wanting to soak up Henry's warmth. "When I first saw the fire, I thought you were dead." Tears streamed down from her vibrant green eyes as Henry wiped every last one away with tender care. "It was Judas who burned the factory," she assumed. "Wasn't it?"

Henry traced the outline of her lower lip. "Yes," he hissed.

"Where is he now?" Elaine shook with fear at the very thought.

"I've been searching for him all day," Henry revealed, casting a glimpse out the window. "Father said that Judas was going back to the island. And he plans to take Louisa with him."

Elaine's eyes widened as she sank her teeth into her bottom lip.

"Listen to me, Elaine." Henry took her face in his hands. "I need you to take Mother and Louisa to the house in the country. Watch over Lilly. You will all be safe there."

Elaine shook her head and sobbed. "Henry, I can't."

"Yes, you can," he urged. "I will come back for you later, I promise."

Elaine gazed into his eyes and whimpered, "Louisa is gone."

Henry gaped in astonishment and then closed his mouth.

"She went looking for William. That was hours ago."

Henry gritted his teeth and banged his fist against the carriage door.

"Fine then," he eventually growled. "You will take Mother with you."

"Henry, I can't," Elaine repeated, bursting into tears even further.

"And why on earth not?" Henry snapped, growing impatient.

"Because she's dead." Elaine covered her mouth to silence the cry that escaped.

Henry turned his head to the side, thinking he must have heard wrong. "What?"

"After I told her about the fire," Elaine confessed, dragging the heel of her hand across her eyelids, "and your father, she went upstairs by herself. She never cried or said a word." Elaine searched his light brown eyes, for he looked off, failing to meet her gaze. "And then tonight I found her on the floor of their bedroom. She drank herself to death, Henry. There were empty bottles of brandy all around her. And I don't—"

"Just stop." Henry held a hand in the air. "I do not wish to hear anymore."

"I'm sorry, Henry." Elaine clung to him, but he was distant. "I am so sorry."

Henry directed the driver to take them back to the Rochester Mansion.

"What about Louisa?" Elaine grabbed his shirtsleeve out of affection.

"I will find her," Henry vowed. "No matter how long it takes."

Worried for his life, Elaine drove her fingernails into the bed of her palm.

Then Henry looked down at her and inhaled. "And you will go to the cellar and hide. I will come back for you tonight with Louisa. Then we will go to the house in the country."

"Cellar—what? But Henry, I don't understand," Elaine protested.

"There is a cellar downstairs in the mansion," Henry explained. "We use it to store wine. You will hide there while I look for Louisa. I can't risk you going home alone in the night, even in a carriage with a driver. Judas is out there." He looked out the window. "I can feel it."

"Why did he do it?" Elaine inquired. "Why did Judas burn down the factory?"

"To make it look like an accident, I suppose." Henry clenched his teeth and smoldered at the memory of blood smeared across his father's face. "He found the treasure, Elaine."

Elaine furrowed her brow. "Why not just take the treasure and go? Why did he take the time to destroy the factory and kill your father?"

"So there would be no witness," Henry answered. "Judas never anticipated that I would be there." Henry sat in silence for a moment, mulling the current events over in his mind. "Perhaps a simple robbery is not in his nature," he figured.

"What about the rest of the treasure? He must

know that was not all of it."

"He knows," Henry said. "Why do you think he burned the place to the ground? It wasn't just a matter of covering up the murder." Henry exhaled. "It was vengeance."

Elaine turned quiet and rested her head on Henry's chest, closing her eyes. She did not know how long she would have to wait until she saw him again. That is, if he survived the night.

"I never should have taken that treasure," Henry admitted.

Elaine sat up in the seat and glanced over at him. "What?"

"It is the only reason he has returned." Henry hung his head and ran his fingers through his hair. "Because we took what belonged to him."

"Henry, that was stolen treasure to begin with. Don't blame yourself for—"

"We may have escaped that island, Elaine. But it will never escape us."

The carriage rolled to a stop as Elaine studied Henry's features with the interest and dedication of a skilled painter. There were furrowing lines of worry etched into his forehead and around the sides of his eyes. A flood of tears resurfaced, and Elaine's vision grew blurry. But Henry dragged her out of the carriage and into the mansion anyway.

"Where is Marge?" He grabbed ahold of Elaine's wrist and slammed the front door behind them.

"She left to visit family for the week. Her

daughter just had a baby."

When Henry let go of Elaine and hustled up the staircase, her heart sank into the pit of her stomach. She chased after him, wanting to protect him from the pain. But she couldn't.

By the time Elaine reached the top of the steps, Henry had already walked into the master bedroom. Elaine followed him inside, where he crouched down by the body of his mother, muffling a belligerent sob with a pair of large hands. Henry was weeping.

"Henry." Elaine touched the top of his shoulder. But Henry jerked away and rose to his feet, fleeing the scene as swiftly as possible. "Henry!" Elaine yelled after him.

Moving as fast as his feet would carry him, Henry bolted down the staircase and searched the main floor of the house for any warm bodies that may have remained. When Elaine reached him, Henry opened a secret passage at the back of the house and pulled her down the narrow steps to the cellar.

"Henry, you must speak to me!" Elaine protested, for he was scaring her.

"You will stay down here." Henry found a lantern in the closet and lit it imperceptibly. "Promise me that you will not leave. Promise me that you will wait for me."

"Let me go with you," Elaine begged. "Please."

Henry tilted his head back and lifted his chin in the air. Then he brushed the back of his knuckles against either of her cheeks, as she closed her eyes and absorbed the touch.

"To think that all of this might have been avoided," Henry whispered. "Mother would still be alive. Father would still be alive. Louisa wouldn't have run off. If only I hadn't taken that treasure. How different all of our lives might have been," he mused, as a lonely teardrop descended his lean, handsome face, softly gliding against his cheekbone.

Elaine leaned her forehead against Henry's, as he shut his eyes and threaded his fingers through her hair. His hands trailed the length of her arms before he grasped her chin and lifted her face so that she was looking right into his eyes. As Elaine opened her mouth to speak, Henry covered her lips with a passionate kiss that was laced with fear and desire.

Trembling at the delicate touch, Elaine curled her arms around his back and sealed her mouth over his. Henry smoothed his fingertips along the curve of Elaine's neck and tugged at her supple skin, claiming and inhaling and cherishing her. When they broke apart, Henry turned away and clambered up the staircase with tears in his eyes.

"Henry, don't leave," she cried. "Please. Take me with you."

As Elaine hurried up the steps after him, Henry made it out the door first and shut it behind him, swiftly clicking the lock in place. Thickly swallowing, Henry disregarded the sound of her screams and weaved his way through the mansion until he was out the front door. Henry could very well die on his mission to find his sister tonight. Locking Elaine away in the cellar was the only way he would know she was safe.

He had done the right thing.

But as Henry stepped out into the night, he wondered if he had made a mistake.

Chapter 9

Louisa ran into a dark alley beneath the taxing blanket of summer rain. As thunder rumbled in the distance, she ducked down behind a dumpster and covered her head with her hands. She had seen the factory on her ride to the mansion this morning. It was then that an unsettling feeling took root in the pit of her soul. Had William done all this?

The rain came down in sheets, so Louisa stared at the dirty ground and resented every hour of wasted time she had encountered today. She had yet to find William. She had yet to find Henry. And she had left Elaine and Mrs. Rochester to reckon with tragedy alone.

When the weather began to calm, a stray dog approached, sniffing at scraps of food on the ground. The mutt reeked of dirt and sweat, a pungent wet dog smell. But Louisa found comfort in the sight of the creature. It was a reminder that she wasn't alone.

Suddenly, someone whistled in the distance, and the dog lifted his head and ears in response. His muddy brown tail wagged back and forth as he placed one paw in front of the other, slowly moving towards that high-pitched noise. When the dog disappeared into the darkness, Louisa sat back on the heel of her hand, afraid of the shadows.

A gun shot sounded and the dog cried, a final, fleeting whimper that echoed in the alleyway. Louisa pressed the flat of her back against the brick wall behind her and crumpled the fabric of her dress in her hand. Her chest rose and fell with each rapid breath, as Louisa shut her eyes tightly, hoping that would make it all go away.

At the sound of heavy footsteps, Louisa lifted her head and looked up into a pair of striking gray eyes. The man they belonged to took a step closer and Louisa screamed.

* * *

Angry with Henry, Elaine paced back and forth in the cellar. How dare he lock her away and reduce the capacity to fend for herself? Elaine kicked the wall and groaned, determined to find a way out of here. In the jungle, Elaine had been all the more capable than Henry. Why must she cower to the level of a weak, lowly woman in the city?

Plotting in her head, Elaine pondered over her present disposition with wonder. Then inspiration struck and she searched the cellar for a piece of wood. Rage surfaced as she carried on with her plan. How dare Henry leave her here without a weapon to defend herself! He could have at least had the sense to supply her with a gun.

When she found a wooden pillar on the ground, excitement chilled her veins. Elaine jerked the pillar up and marched up the staircase, ready and willing to flee. Using both arms, she thrust the piece of wood into the door again and again.

Resentment and mourning coiled around each other and hardened her heart, aiding the current task at hand. Once Elaine had made enough of an impact, she kicked the door in and busted through. Triumphant at last, Elaine tossed the wooden pillar aside and grabbed ahold of the doorframe until she had worked her way back into the house.

But once Elaine stepped onto the main floor, her body froze at the sound of laughter. For Judas was standing on the other side of the door, waiting for her.

Elaine ran for the front entrance of the house, but Judas caught the skirt of her dress and tugged. When Elaine tripped, she hit her head on the edge of an end table and collapsed to the ground. Judas planted a boot on either side of her waist as he towered above her. "I seem to be having some trouble finding your dear sister-in-law," he revealed. "Do you have any idea where she may be? Where she might have run off to?"

"No." Elaine glowered up at him with malice

and hatred in her eyes.

Judas smiled, looking off. Then he leaned down and slapped her across the face. Turning her head to the side, Elaine coughed and tasted blood along her lip.

"Now," Judas huffed. "I'm going to beg your forgiveness and ask you again."

"No. I will never tell you where she is." Elaine reared up and spit in his face.

Wiping his brow, Judas straddled her waist and wrapped his hands around her throat. Elaine bucked and writhed beneath him, clawing at his arms in protest.

"Fine." Judas released her as she struggled to catch her breath. "If I cannot take Louisa with me, then I'll just take you instead." Judas stood and snatched her up.

"NO!" Elaine shrieked, fighting against him.

Judas picked her up in his arms and dragged her through the house. She kicked and screamed, digging her nails into his flesh. When Judas dropped her down to the floor, her body felt bruised and broken.

Elaine glanced up at him from the flat of her back, her mouth hanging wide open, for all the breath had left her lungs. Judas turned her over and wrapped his arms around her stomach, jerking Elaine to her own two feet. Then he slammed the side of her head into the wall until she was knocked out cold.

* * *

After traveling through the city by carriage proved unsuccessful, Henry sent the driver home and took off on foot. While it seemed wise earlier, the decision appeared to be anything but clever, now that Henry was stuck out in the middle of a storm. His long dark locks were dripping wet and his clothes were soaked through.

The hunt for Louisa left him circling the town, as Henry found himself back at the Rochester Mansion. Once he entered the front door, Henry slowed at the first sign of an intruder. A trail of evidence led him to the cellar door, whose gaping hole boasted that a beast must have shoveled its way inside.

At the horrendous sight, Henry felt all of the breath drift away from his body. He staggered back and slammed into the wall, slowly sinking down to the floor. Henry tore his fingers through his hair and pounded his knuckles against his head.

Guilt. That was all Henry claimed and all Henry felt.

In the hope of saving them both, he had left his wife in pursuit of his sister. Now they were both gone. Essentially, Henry's search had amassed to nothing.

An object glimmered out of the corner of his eye, as Henry spotted something gold on the floor. It was Elaine's wedding band. The sight of it turned his stomach upside down.

Henry picked the ring up and placed his finger and thumb through either side of the circle. Suddenly, it occurred to him what Mr. Rochester had said this morning. Some of his father's final words.

Judas was going back to the island and planned to take Louisa with him. But what if he hadn't been able to find her? What if Judas had come to the mansion looking for Louisa but then left with Elaine instead?

Henry rose to his feet at the possibility and slipped the ring in his pocket. Following his instincts, he headed to the front door and barged out into the night. Once he reached the sidewalk, Henry crossed the street and looked across the way at the harbor.

His heart pounded inside of his chest when he saw a ship with black sails and a white flower centered in the middle of the fabric. Utterly alarmed, Henry took off running for the docks, not minding if he happened to break his foot on the way. The throbbing pulse point in his neck was nothing to the icy fear freezing his veins from the inside out.

Once he reached the edge of the docks, Henry stopped to catch his breath. With his hands on his waist, Henry watched Judas in the distance, forcing Elaine onto the ship. Her hands were tied in front of her, while Judas had a tight grip on her arm with his hand. Henry clenched his teeth at the sight and waited for them to disappear below deck. Then he ran across the bordering dock and dove into the water.

Henry moved his arms about as he pushed through the sea, his eyes burning at the salty sting. Stroke after stroke, he propelled himself forward until he reached the ship. Once Henry kicked himself to the surface, he smoothed his wet hair back out of his face and silently breathed aloud. From where he floated, not a sound was heard onboard.

Catching his breath, Henry noticed a dangling rope over the side of the ship. Though its presence appeared too good to be true, Henry grabbed ahold of the rope and began his slow ascent. Resilient, he pulled at the rope as his boots touched the side of the ship.

In silent arrival, Henry crouched down on the deck and dragged the rope up from the ocean, dropping it down beside his feet. Stealthy in the moonlight, Henry peered into an open entryway and proceeded onto the ship. It was there he found a young woman tied and gagged in the corner. Only the woman wasn't Elaine. It was Louisa.

"Louisa," Henry gasped, rushing towards her.

After removing the gag from her mouth, Henry pulled a pocket knife out and proceeded to cut the rope binding her hands and feet. Speechless, his poor sister was cold, wet, and shaking, in too much of a state of shock to handle the situation.

"Who brought you here, Louisa?" Henry

touched her head.

"I don't know," she mumbled, rubbing her palms against her arms.

"Was it William?" he wondered, checking over his shoulder for him.

"No." Louisa pulled her knees into her chest and studied the wooden boards beneath her. "It was a man I have never seen before in my entire life."

"What did he look like?" Henry prodded. "I need you to be specific."

"He had eyes," she began, shaken and stuttering. "Gray eyes. Auburn hair."

"And what of Elaine?" Henry tilted her chin up and felt the icy coolness of her skin. "Have you seen her? Have you seen Elaine? Have you seen my wife?"

"Yes." Louisa looked off in the distance, as if she were staring at something that was not there. Something invisible. Something toxic. Something dangerous. "He put her in a cage."

"What?" Henry rocked back on his heels, thinking he had misheard.

"He put her in a cage, Henry," she repeated. "Like an animal."

Chapter 10

E laine sat down and wrapped her arms around herself, feeling the cool metal bars of the cage through the thin gown over her body. Judas had removed all of her other clothes the moment he trapped her below deck, even taking great lengths to strip away her socks and shoes. She was cold and frightened, wondering how he could have possibly come back.

"Are you hungry?" Judas taunted her from a distance, sitting in an old wooden chair.

Biting on her lower lip, Elaine rested her chin over her knees as the length of her gown brushed over her feet. She understood the symbolic nature of the cage, and the message Judas intended to send by it. Elaine had once been imprisoned on the island with Jade.

When Elaine failed to respond, Judas approached the cage and forced a slab of raw meat through one of the holes. The smell made her toes curl and her jaw clench, as she held her tongue and looked away. There was blood on the meat and a growing swarm of flies. Elaine cringed at the mere thought of it next to her and held on to one of the metal bars for support.

"Have you turned soft during your time in the city?" Judas asked. "How disappointing of you, Elaine. I would have thought an island girl like you would—"

Elaine glanced up at Judas and he ceased speaking, staring into her eyes.

"You always were enchanting," he cadenced. "Especially those eyes."

Elaine lowered her gaze at the sound of his words, hopeless and miserable.

"What color would you call them?" Judas teased. "Green, I imagine."

The ship jolted forward, as Elaine recognized the sudden shift in movement. A sinister smile pealed across Judas's face at the sight of her fear, although she was really more surprised. Someone else was on the ship.

"What do you want?" Elaine grew bold enough to say. Her back ached and her breasts were filled with milk that her helpless newborn would go without. Regardless, of all the many things she felt for Judas, submission was not one of them.

Judas cocked his head to the side and regarded her amicably.

"You've stolen the treasure, burned down the factory and murdered my father-in-law. What more could you possibly want from my family?"

Elaine hissed, filled with malevolence.

"You always have amused me, island girl," he replied with a subtle laugh.

When Judas rose to his feet and paced the floor in front of her, she loathed the hierarchy of power at play. While she remained seated with her knees buckled and head bowed, Judas hovered above Elaine in an upright position, towering over her to a much greater advantage than the mere difference in height would allow. He wanted control.

"When you left the island, you took the treasure with you," he announced. "But not all of it." Judas settled his steady blue gaze on hers, hoping to lure her further. "Samson and Peter have hidden the rest throughout the island. You will help me find it."

"Why? You don't know where it is?" she teased, challenging him.

With a snicker, Judas knelt down in front of the cage and rested his head against the metal bars. "You lived in that godforsaken jungle longer than I can imagine."

Elaine slowly closed and opened her eyes, acknowledging the truth.

"You know that island better than any man," he declared, offering her a surprising compliment. "You're the only one who can help me find it."

Elaine thought the proposition over. "Why should I trust you? Even if I do as you say, if I help you find the treasure, you'll just kill me afterwards anyway. Why bother?"

"Clever girl." Judas shook his finger at her and raised an eyebrow. "How does this sound? If you don't do as I say, I will kill you, and your husband, and his sister, and that precious little daughter of yours as well. Does that clear up the confusion?"

Elaine shut her mouth and swallowed, hanging her head in defeat.

"Philip was just the beginning," Judas warned. "That batty mother-in-law of yours could very well be next. Now, how would your husband take to that?"

Elaine watched him with a smug smile. "Quite easily, considering she's already dead." As Judas furrowed his brow in confusion, Elaine continued, "She drank herself to death after I told her what happened to Philip. Would you like to take credit for her death as well?"

Squaring his shoulders, Judas guessed, "Bottle of whiskey?"

"Brandy," she clarified, taking particular delight in his ignorance.

"I see." Judas rose to his feet and grabbed the chair, planting it right before the cage. When he took a seat, Judas reached out and clung to the metal bars.

"What if I made you a deal?" Elaine suggested.

"Oh, I like the sound of that." Judas leaned down and grabbed a bottle of rum off the floor. "What kind of deal, island girl?" He removed the cork and took a long swig, wiping the back of his hand across his mouth like a drunken savage.

"In exchange for the safety of Louisa, Henry, and my child," she propositioned. "You will leave each of them unharmed. Not so much as touch a hair on any of their heads."

Judas sucked on the bottle of rum. "And what will I receive in return?"

Elaine's long black hair fell down around her face. "Me," she whispered.

"You?" He laughed at the idea, taking another long pull. "What benefit would I get out of you?"

"Whatever you want," she offered. "I can do whatever you want, be whatever you want. You can do whatever you want to me, and I won't complain. You can even kill me."

"Ha!" He slapped his thigh and scratched the stubble along his jaw. "Why would I kill you?" he questioned. "I believe you would serve me much better alive, island girl."

"Perhaps," Elaine mused, fluttering her dark lashes at him.

"Didn't anyone ever tell you not to strike a bargain with the devil?" he asked.

"I suppose not," Elaine replied. "I must have missed church that week."

Judas chuckled at her humor, standing up and leaning against the cage.

Elaine smiled with delight, charming Judas with those exotic green eyes. He had fallen prey to them from the moment he first saw her. A convenient detail that she would undoubtedly rely on for leverage as long as he held her prisoner.

"Well then, I do believe we have a deal." Judas stuck his hand through the bars, his wrist dangling against the cage. Appearing all the more brave, Elaine extended her hand and when Judas took it, she looked into his eyes and relaxed.

"So long as you hold your end of the bargain, I shall hold mine," she vowed.

"Excellent." Judas scraped his nails over the bed of her palm and squeezed, while Elaine remained still as a statue and let him. "That reminds me." As he pulled his hand through the bars, Elaine relaxed into the back of the cage with relief. "I have something to show you. Something that I believe you will be delighted to see."

Elaine bit her tongue and swallowed. "Marvelous," she chimed with a placid smile.

Judas set the bottle of rum on the floor and walked backwards. "I shall return." With a deep chuckle, he cupped his hands to his mouth, patronizing her. "Don't go anywhere!"

Pleased with his disappearance, Elaine rested the back of her head against the cage and closed her eyes. She worried for Lilly. She worried for Henry. She worried for Louisa.

Despite the danger, Elaine believed the deal she had made with the devil would prove worthwhile. She had more resilience in her than Judas knew. A pillaging pirate such as himself had little time for patience or virtue. But patience might have been Elaine's most potent virtue of all.

"Oh, island girl," Judas called, though Elaine refused to open her eyes just yet. "I have a gift for you," he sing-songed. "A way to make our deal official."

Deep within the pit of her soul, Elaine knew that she would be wiser to keep her eyes shut. But there was a pressing need to see whatever he had brought near. So she fluttered her lashes as if she had momentarily dozed off, appearing dreamy and seductive.

"What have you brought for me, William?" Elaine sweetly wondered.

"A gift," he repeated. "A gift for you." He approached the cage. "Only you." Judas wrapped his fingers around a set of perpendicular bars on the cage. His other hand remained behind his back, the mystery gift momentarily hidden from sight. "While I appreciate your effort, I would rather you not call me William on La Fleur Noire."

Elaine glanced about the ship in admiration. "How about Captain Pierce?"

"Much better. Just an island girl, yet you are already catching on." Judas patronized her by holding the gift hostage behind his back. "Now," he finally said. "Would you like to see?"

Elaine pursed her lips and nodded. "Of course, Captain Pierce," she cooed.

With an ear-splitting grin, Judas swung his arm in front of the cage and held the gift for Elaine to see. Her eyes deadened at the sight, as she remained imperceptibly calm. Elaine was screaming on the inside, but she would never let him know the way it had affected her. He hardly deserved the satisfaction.

"Well, what do you think?" Judas wanted to know, eager as ever.

"When will we arrive on the island?" She searched his cobalt irises intensely.

Disliking her reaction, Judas set the gift down in the chair directly facing Elaine. "When the seasons change," was his only reply, as he left her alone in the room.

Once he was gone, Elaine crawled on her hands and knees until she reached the front of the cage. Then she clung to the metal bars and quietly wept, careful not to let so much as a random passerby hear. Eventually, Elaine turned silent and simply stared straight ahead.

She stared for a very long time.

The gift waiting for Elaine in the chair was Jade's stuffed head, already prepared for proper wall display. That is, apart from the most alluring aspect of any mounted trophy.

Her eyes were missing.

Chapter 11

At the sound of footsteps, Henry popped his head up and stood before Louisa, protecting her feeble body. When an unfamiliar man stalked towards them, Louisa screamed. It was the stranger from the alleyway with auburn hair and gray eyes.

He grabbed Louisa and Henry by the arm and shoved them into a dark room, locking brother and sister inside. Confined in such close quarters, Henry and Louisa split apart as the former made every attempt to find some way out, kicking and banging at the door. The latter merely trembled in place and cried, wholly shocked in horror.

After every failed attempt, Henry gave out from exhaustion and crumpled to the floor. He ran a frantic hand over his face, plagued with worry for Elaine. Where was Judas keeping her? What had he done to her? What did he plan to do to her?

"Henry," Louisa whimpered, shivering with

fear. "I'm frightened."

With a heavy sigh, Henry rose to his feet and trudged towards his sister in the dark. When he made out her image in the corner, Henry crouched down beside her and curled his arm around her shoulder. "Everything is going to be all right, Louisa."

Turning into his warmth, Louisa buried her head in Henry's chest and wept. "Elaine was right," she cried. "William is not the man I thought he was. I never knew him at all."

Henry rubbed her arm and tucked her head beneath his chin, holding her close in the night. She was fragile and shaken, but his thoughts helplessly returned to Elaine at every moment. His greatest fear was that he may never be able to touch her again.

"What is his name?" Louisa wondered, clinging to Henry. "His real name?"

Henry clenched his jaw and swallowed. "Judas," he revealed. "He's a pirate, Louisa."

"P-Pirate?" She struggled to get the word out, her teeth clacking together.

"Yes," Henry hissed, though in a gentle enough tone not to frighten her. "A pirate and a killer. Judas murdered Elaine's father years ago. Once, he even tried to kill her."

Louisa bowed her head and let the tears come crashing down like a thunderstorm. Her trembling fingers dabbed at the moisture around her eyes. "No, Henry," she croaked. "No."

"I am sorry, sweet Louisa." Henry rubbed her back to comfort her. "Truly, I am."

Eventually, Louisa got ahold of herself and dried her eyes. As she leaned against the sturdy wall behind them, reality flashed across her pretty pale face. "It was a lie."

Henry folded his palms together and stared at the floor.

"All of it," Louisa realized. "Every moment of our courtship, Henry." She turned to him and tugged at his collar. "He was no more in love with me than—than..."

"You were a pawn, Louisa," Henry remarked. "I'm sorry to be so cruel, but it is the truth. You have no fault in the matter, dear sister. Do not blame yourself."

"How can I do anything but blame myself?" Louisa threaded her fingers through her blonde locks and yanked. "I liked him. I brought him to the house. And now Mother and Father are—" She broke down again, sniffling and sobbing. "I thought he loved me."

"Shh..." Henry pulled her close and stroked his fingers through her hair. "He did not love you, indeed. He chose you. It is clear to me now how well he must have had everything planned. I never imagined that he would come back."

"Come back?" Louisa turned her chin up and watched her brother.

"Yes. We first encountered Judas on the island. When we left, he was dead."

"Dead?" Louisa brushed the back of her hand against her eyelids.

"Elaine killed him," Henry murmured. "Plunged a dagger straight into his heart."

Louisa shook her head in confusion. "But how can that be? How can he—?"

"I do not know." Henry stared off in the darkness. "It is a mystery."

Exhaling aloud, Louisa relaxed her shoulders and fluttered her shimmering blue eyes about the room. Could it be true? William a pirate? A murderer? A ghost?

Henry sighed and rested the back of his head against the wall, folding his arms across the tops of his knees. As the ship jostled against the waves, Henry felt the motion and understood its significance. If only he could push the anxiety and fear from his mind.

"Henry..." Louisa whimpered, turning to face him. "Where are we going?"

Blowing warm air through his nostrils, Henry acknowledged her in the shadows.

"Where is William taking us?" She clutched his arms and held on tight.

Hating to be the bearer of bad news, he took a breath and sighed, "To the island."

Chapter 12

Weeks passed that felt like months. Months that felt like years. Elaine suffered the painful reality of leaving her newborn without mother's milk. The bond she had longed for them to share would never be formed. A silent tear skittered down her cheek at the thought. But when Judas entered the room, she softly swiped it away.

Another man slithered into the room alongside Judas. His hair was wavy and thick, hanging just above his shoulders, a pretty auburn color which brought attention to his strong, masculine nature. With freckled skin and light eyes, he hardly looked as menacing as Judas. But the man was taller, wider, a broad-shouldered athlete fit for a battleground or coliseum. No wonder Judas had kept him so close.

"Frederic," Judas snapped, crossing his arms over his chest as he clenched his jaw with the word.

Averting his eyes, Frederic retrieved a large

hoop-like key ring from his pocket and opened the lock on the cage. When the door made of metal bars swung open, Frederic returned the clacking set of iron keys to his pocket and stepped aside. Judas stormed into the cage and bound Elaine's wrists in front of her with rope.

She bit her tongue and closed her eyes when the rope burned against her delicate skin. Once he was finished, Judas pushed her raven black locks over either of her shoulders. His hand settled along the side of her throat, and she turned away at his touch.

Offended by her rejection, Judas grabbed her hair and pulled until her head jerked back in response. Elaine gasped, feeling his fingers at the back of her skull. Surely, he could crush it if he so desired.

"What is the matter, island girl?" he whispered in her ear, breathing down her neck. "Have you forgotten our agreement?"

"No," she spat back at him.

Judas ran his thumb along her jawline and muttered, "You are mine."

Elaine froze beneath his touch and forced down the bile rising in her throat.

Judas grabbed her elbows and dragged her after him. "Get the others," he commanded, turning back to Frederic with a mindful eye.

Elaine's curiosity piqued at the word others. Had Judas captured more while she had been on the boat? When they were in the city?

"Move!" Judas kicked her heels and Elaine gasped, gritting her teeth. She looked back over her shoulder and glared, hating him with every fiber of her being.

But Judas merely tightened his grip and pushed her forward. With the way he controlled the angle of her body, Elaine could have tripped over her own two feet on her way up the stairs. Not that Judas would have any pity on her.

Once the first rays of sunshine came into view above deck, Elaine relaxed her shoulders and looked up at the beautiful blue sky. It had been so long since she had felt the cool breeze on her cheeks, the warm sun on her face. But as Judas gripped the tether of rope hanging from her wrists and yanked, Elaine's eyes settled on the lush paradise ahead.

It was the island she had left long ago. The same island she had once called home. Despite the truth of probability and chance, they were back.

Judas set his arm along the small of Elaine's back and hauled her off the ship. She took a hesitant breath with every step, but let Judas guide her to the sand. Once her feet scrubbed against the muddy ground, Elaine smiled down at her toes. It had been so long since she had felt the gritty texture, but it was a welcome sensation nonetheless.

"Stand up straight. Shoulders back." Judas slapped her arm in dominance.

"Whatever for," Elaine retorted, resisting the controlling command.

"Because I told you to." Judas touched her cheek. "Island girl."

Grimacing at the feel of his finger, Elaine straightened her posture and did as he said. Deep down, she knew that it had been an awful mistake to have an agreement with Judas, to make a deal with the devil. But she could rely on some comfort in the truth that Lilly, Henry and Louisa were all safe in New York, carefully tucked away from harm.

Elaine preferred to be the one taken hostage by Judas any day of the week. No matter how tortuous these months had been apart from her family, nothing mattered more than their safety. As long as her daughter was safe. As long as her husband was safe. As long as her sister was safe. She could handle anything that Judas threw her way.

"The others," Frederic announced, strolling off the ship with Henry and Louisa in tow.

Elaine's jaw dropped as her eyes widened in fear. All this time, the two loved ones she was most concerned with protecting were here. On the ship. Held captive. Just like her.

When she turned back to Judas, he laughed, amused by her agony.

"You told me they would be safe. You promised no harm would come to them."

"And you believed me," Judas murmured.

"You believed a pirate. Imagine that."

Scowling with fury, Elaine lifted her bound wrists and went to slam them down on top of Judas's head. But before she could make contact, he snatched her up by the arm and squeezed tight. Painfully tight. She bucked and fought against him in defiance, but it was no use.

"Let me go!" Elaine scowled, loathing the very sight of him.

Judas released his grip on her arm only to slap her across the face and kick her in the stomach until she flew back and tumbled to the ground. When Elaine dug her elbows into the sand for support, she leaned over heaving, for Judas had knocked the wind right out of her. Her jaw throbbed and she tasted blood along the corner of her mouth. One thing was for certain, during the hunt for treasure on the island, Judas would not be gentle.

"Elaine!" Henry cried out, squirming to work his way out of Frederic's hold.

Elaine lifted her head to take in the sight of her husband and sister-in-law, both approaching on either side of Frederic with their hands in chains. The sun was at high noon, that big orange ball floating over a tapestry of blue sky. The blinding light made Elaine squint her eyes, as she tried to imagine a situation worse than the one they were already in.

"Take her." Judas nodded towards Louisa, though his eyes remained on Frederic. "Take the girl."

"You will not touch her!" Henry declared, his chest rising and falling from all the excitement. His smooth dark locks had grown longer during their time at sea, skirting past his shoulders now. In truth, everyone's hair had lengthened over the past few months apart from Judas. The realization did not sit well with Elaine. Judas had a knife.

"No." Judas cocked his head to the side. "But he will."

Frederic grasped Louisa's small arm and took her away, pulling her behind him as her bare feet dragged across the sand. Elaine hung her head and cried, while Henry leapt forward to chase after them. But Judas tripped Henry and then punched him in the gut, a severe blow to the abdomen, even for someone of Henry's strength and stamina.

Elaine longed to rise to her feet and defend them both, but the impact from the kick to her stomach had not lessened. She could hardly get her breath back, much less stand. And without the use of her hands, any attempt to fend him off would prove futile.

"What is he going to do to her?" Henry sat back on his knees and looked up at the blonde devil, wishing that he could crush his jaw with his bare hands.

To be mocking, Judas crouched down before Henry and pulled at the front of his hair so he was forced to stare into those sinister cobalt eyes.

"Whatever he wishes to."

Henry clenched his jaw as Judas released him, rising up and taking a cautious step back. For a moment, those blue eyes turned kind and innocent. Elaine sank into the sand and watched the scene unfold, not knowing what to expect. But then Judas grinned far too wide for Elaine's content.

"NO!" She screamed as Judas punched Henry in the jaw.

It was a rough hit, coldcocking Henry like that, though neither should have been surprised. Elaine crawled on her hands and knees until she reached Judas, understanding that she had to do something. But Judas had no mercy, repeatedly pounding his fist against Henry's face, in an attempt to disrupt his beautiful features, his alluring looks, every bit of what made his appearance a handsome one.

Blood dribbled down Henry's chin, a pitiful shade of red against his pearly whites. His eyes fell shut when the skin around them began to swell, and Elaine worried that Judas was not going to stop, that the intention was to kill him.

With all the strength she could muster, Elaine got a running start and leapt onto Judas's back, knocking him in the head with her balled up fists. But Judas tossed her off his back and onto the ground in no time, kicking her in the spleen for good measure. Elaine doubled over in pain and cried out, reaching her hands towards Henry.

His beautiful face was a matted canvas of sagging, puffy flesh sopped in fluid and blood. Elaine held a palm to her mouth, weeping at the harsh brutality of the torture Judas planned to inflict. Her greatest fear was that the violence had only just begun.

"STOP!" Elaine whimpered, dragging her feeble body to Judas's feet. She got down on her knees and batted her long dark lashes up at him, revealing those resilient green eyes that captivated him even now. "Take me," she begged. "You can have me."

"No!" Henry barked, wheezing from the shortness of breath in his lungs.

"Please." Elaine tugged at Judas's trousers, charming him with the coy look in her eyes. "Take me. Leave him alone, and you can have me," she repeated. "You can touch me."

Judas moistened his lips with his tongue and gazed down with satisfaction at the sight of her dropping to her knees before him. "You will leave your husband for me?"

It took everything in her not to tear her gaze away and look at Henry for the last time. But she had to keep eye contact with the monster. So she stared lovingly into his eyes and whispered, "Yes."

"NO!" Henry groaned, lunging for Judas. But the latter kicked him in the jaw and Henry flew back to the ground with no way of regaining himself.

With Henry taken care of, Judas glanced down

at the beautiful creature before him and held out his open hand, dirty and scarred. Elaine swallowed and pressed her palm against his, letting him feel of her soft skin and squeeze. Her heart throbbed loudly and painfully against her bones, because she did not want him. No other had ever been destined to touch her than her husband, but her body was the only leverage she had. So she took it.

Judas rubbed both of Elaine's forearms and helped her to her feet. Her glistening green eyes never seemed to blink as he stared into the depths of her soul. From instinct alone, he lifted his hand and cupped her cheek in his palm. Her golden complexion mesmerized him until there was tingling in his fingertips.

The wind came rushing in and swept Elaine's black locks around her face. Judas tucked a strand of glossy hair behind her ear and dragged his thumb along her jawline, a surprisingly delicate gesture for the man in question. As if under a spell, Judas parted his lips and lowered his face to meet her eyes.

Elaine sank her teeth into her lower lip and watched Judas's eyes slide shut with the intention of a sweet kiss. But the second before his mouth met hers, Elaine ground her teeth together and slammed her knee into his groin with as much force as possible. Judas yelped in pain, so she capitalized on the rare moment of opportunity and took action. Elaine clamped her fists together as if they were gripping a baseball bat and pounded them against the side of his face until she connected with his ear.

Judas tumbled over and crashed to the ground like Goliath. Breathing heavily, he looked about the place as if he did not recognize where he was. Henry crept up beside him and sliced his face with the shackles around his wrists. When blood sprang to the surface of Judas's skin, his eyes rolled back into his head and he crumpled to the sand in a state of unconsciousness.

Running across the sand, Henry darted into the jungle with Elaine at his heels. Even though each lacked the use of their hands, the couple tore through the forest with wrists bound, determined to reach the deepest part of the jungle and hide.

Birds ascended from tree branches and flew to the sky at the intrusion of Henry and Elaine in their secret paradise. When Elaine tripped over a rut in the ground, Henry turned back and helped her to her feet. It would have been wise to pause for an instant to catch one's breath, but Henry and Elaine had no time for the practical and ideal.

The jungle floor felt anything but soft against the bottom of their feet. But Elaine persevered, even when a painful object dug into her heel. Henry suffered similar discomfort along the soles of his feet, but with the pain scorching and searching across his face, he could hardly think of the countless injuries brewing elsewhere.

When they reached the waterfall, Elaine stumbled to her knees gasping for breath. She reached her arms out and dragged her body to the edge of the lagoon, where she dipped her head into the cool water and opened her mouth for a series of long drinks.

Looking back over his shoulder, Henry brushed the palms of his hands against his trousers and knelt down beside Elaine. With his hands equally bound, Henry followed suit and dropped his face to the clear pane of fresh liquid. When his lips met the water, Henry sucked down mouthful after mouthful so quickly that he thought he might be sick.

Once Elaine had her fill, she sprawled her legs out on the bank and breathed a sigh of relief. Her thirst had been quenched, but if only that had been the most pressing matter at the moment. Elaine looked around in the jungle and could not deny the feeling that she was at home. But then Henry pulled back from the lagoon and turned to face her.

"Elaine," Henry gasped, locking eyes with the love of his life.

At the sound of her name on his lips, Elaine inched forward and placed her head on his chest. She listened to his steady heartbeat as Henry placed kisses along the side of her face and up and down her neck. If neither of their hands were bound, they could have held each other close. Since that was not the case, they embraced in the best way they possibly could.

Elaine pressed her forehead to Henry's and

closed her eyes. "Henry, I—"

"He is never going to touch you, Elaine," he rasped. "Do you understand me?"

Pulling back to gaze into his light brown eyes, Elaine looked over his battered face and whimpered. "Henry, I thought it was just me on the ship. If I had known—"

"Shh..." Henry cooed, touching her face the best he could with his hands bound. "If you had been taken before I reached the ship, I wouldn't have been able to bear it."

Elaine leaned in and crushed her lips to his, then kissed the tender bruises on his face. She would have done anything in her power to make them vanish forever. Just like she hoped Judas would one day disappear from their lives for good. Today was not that day.

"We must hide," Elaine eventually said. "Later we will find him and attack."

Henry nodded, finding nothing but sense in the preemptive plan. When he sat up on his knees and squirmed, Elaine did not know what to make of the look on his face.

"There is a knife in my pocket," Henry revealed. "Take it, Elaine."

Obeying at once, Elaine reached one of her bound hands into his pocket and wrapped her fingers around the knife. Then she handed the blade to Henry, and he forced her palms together the best he could. Despite the shackles, Henry gripped the knife in his left hand and began sawing away at the tough rope that kept Elaine restrained.

"Why would he tie my hands with rope, but have you put in chains?" she asked.

Henry kept his eyes on the task at hand, determined to free Elaine.

A gunshot sounded in the distance, echoing through the jungle.

Elaine snapped her head back, her green eyes searching every thicket, every crevice, every vine. She felt hollow and weak all at once, the blood mercilessly draining from her face. When she regained her breathing, Elaine turned to face Henry and quivered.

"Louisa," Elaine whispered. "Where is Louisa?"

Henry gulped as his knife cut through the final strand of rope binding her wrists. His jaw trembled with fear at the probability of what had happened. "In the jungle."

Chapter 13

Frederic clasped Louisa's arm and pulled as her heels dragged against the sand. Begging for mercy, she looked back over her shoulder until the faint image of Henry and Elaine in the distance was no more. From afar, she had witnessed what William had done to her brother. All the while, she could not fathom how he could be capable of savage violence and brutality. William had been a kind, caring, affectionate gentleman in New York.

But now, Louisa struggled to cope with the painful truth. Who had burned the factory? Murdered her father? Kidnapped her? Taken them all prisoner?

William. The man she loved.

"NO!" Louisa shrieked when Frederic took her into the jungle. She stared straight ahead, observing the large muscular nature of his figure. Fredcric was tall and strong, a full grown man. She was small and petite, with no hope of fighting him off. Against the male dominance Frederic had the capacity to exude, Louisa never stood a chance.

Understanding her fate, Louisa struggled to keep up with Frederic's pounding pace as he trekked through the jungle. But then Frederic spotted a smooth slab of rock and forced Louisa to take a seat. The moment her posterior connected with the hard surface, Frederic clamped his hand over her mouth to silence her screams.

"Be quiet," Frederic hissed.

Louisa closed her eyes for a moment and felt the rough callouses of his hand against her lips. His nostrils flared with the intake of breath. Especially considering what he was about to do to her.

Rape. Assault. Murder. Surely, that was what the stranger had in mind. Perhaps he was a sadist as well, deriving pleasure from all the many ways he could see her suffer.

"Would you stop shaking?" Frederic watched her with careful eyes, slowly withdrawing his hand from her mouth.

Louisa sat stock still on the stone, regarding him with amazement when he showed no intention to strike her. Instead, Frederic knelt down and slipped his hand into his trouser pocket. After removing an iron key ring, he sorted through them all before finding the one to fit Louisa's lock.

"What are you doing?" Louisa crooned, her veins surging with adrenaline and fear.

Frederic stared up at her for a moment, then

lowered his lashes and unlocked the shackles. When they dropped to the ground, Frederic picked the shackles up and tossed them deep into the forest, where they would never be found. "Freeing you," he finally said.

Louisa remained unmoved, unable to believe a word he had said. "Why?"

Not expecting such a response, he furrowed his brow and inquired, "You need a reason?"

"I suppose not," Louisa mused. "But I would like one." When he made no attempt to respond, she said, "How do I know I can trust you?" Louisa got to her feet and smoothed out the folds of her dress. "How do I know you won't hurt me? How do I know you won't come after me?"

Frederic sighed at her slew of questions and replied, "You don't."

Louisa gazed about the forest in bewilderment, her blue eyes fluttering about. Frederic thought they were a pretty shade of blue, soft, yet bright, a striking mixture of sky and sea.

"You are free to go, miss," Frederic declared. "So go."

With her eyes on Frederic, Louisa took a hesitant step back, not quite sure if she could trust his word. At the sound of a gunshot, Louisa froze in her tracks. Frederic widened his eyes and gave her a frantic push.

"Run," Frederic commanded. He shoved her forward when she refused to move. "Go! Run!"

Louisa took off on foot and never looked back.

She ran through the jungle like a frightened child, for that is all she was. Breath left her lungs at a rampant pace, as she pumped her legs and gasped.

Frightened for her life, Louisa ran and ran, striving for the deepest part of the jungle. Once her legs tired, she slowed to a walk, never forgetting the brisk pace. At the sight of a large tree whose girth alluded to the jungle, Louisa touched the bark and sat down to rest.

Everything around her was like a strange new world. Full of creatures and green. So much green. Louisa longed for her father, she longed for her mother, she longed for New York. But now she was a city girl stranded in the jungle. How would she ever survive?

* * *

With Elaine free of the rope that had once bound her wrists, she cupped a generous amount of water in the bed of her palms to wash the blood from Henry's face. There was definite swelling, and the bruising had already begun. But Elaine could hardly believe that he was alive, much less on the same ship as she had been transported on.

While Henry collected his thoughts, Elaine searched through the boulders alongside the waterfall. The same slabs of stone that Jade used to lay across when Elaine bathed. Her protector in the jungle.

The pressing memory felt no more than a day old. But Elaine quickly cast her bitter nostalgia aside, not allowing the pain of her past to affect her future. So she sorted through rocks until she found one heavy enough to break the chain holding Henry's shackles together.

Looking about the forest, Elaine knew they had yet to be discovered. She ambled towards Henry and took his arm to help him up. Understanding her intentions, Henry knelt down before a rough stone slab and pulled his hands apart. The chain between his shackles pulled tight, as Henry gazed up at her in earnest.

"Well," he muttered. "Go ahead."

Elaine held Henry's cautious gaze, but nodded anyway. When she picked up the small boulder with two hands, Henry flexed the muscles in his arms. Elaine's palms were clammy and her body was tired. She didn't trust herself.

Henry caught her eye and sighed, "Elaine."

"I've never done this before," she confessed. "I could break your hand."

Henry looked down at the stone beneath him.

"I could break your arm."

"But you won't," Henry replied. "Now just do it, Elaine. I trust you."

Though she had less faith in herself, Elaine positioned her body at the right angle and lifted the object in the air. Henry held his wrists tight and looked away. Despite the fear rousing up inside of her, Elaine held the boulder over her head and then slammed it down between Henry's hands.

At the clink of metal, Henry froze and lifted his head to look at Elaine. She removed the boulder to see the work it had done. A single link on the chain was broken, yet Henry was far from free.

"Again, Elaine," Henry said. When she stilled before him in hesitation, he repeated, "Again."

Mashing her lips together, Elaine lifted the boulder over her head and brought it down with a cracking blow. But it was still not enough to free Henry from the chains. Once Elaine sighed in defeat, Henry squared his shoulders and stretched his arms as far apart from each other as he could. Understanding him intuitively, Elaine slammed the boulder between his hands one last time. It was then that the chain broke and Henry finally regained free use of his arms.

Elaine set the boulder on the ground and leaned over Henry to inspect the marks on either of his wrists. The metal cuffs were gone, and his hands were finally free. Henry touched Elaine's forearm and looked into her beautiful green eyes, the windows to her soul, the only woman he had ever loved. His wife.

Desperate to hold her, Henry clutched her chin in his hand and then stroked his fingers along her jawline. Elaine shut her eyes at the sensitive contact, because it had been so long since someone held her close. As Henry leaned forward and brought his mouth to hers, a shrill scream echoed through the wilderness. A terrified scream.

A feminine scream. Louisa's scream.

Henry grabbed Elaine and pulled her behind him as they scurried through the jungle. Quiet and careful footsteps were all they could take to keep from making their presence known. They ducked behind trees at any sound, though it always proved to be the noise of a creature, the only music in the jungle.

Once they returned to the beach, Henry firmly clutched the knife in his hand. Elaine dropped her arms at her sides and searched the sand and sea in bewilderment. Her eyes raced all about, but she found no evidence that Judas had ever been there.

"Where is he?" Elaine turned in a circle and stripped her fingers through her hair. Her breathing slowed to a pace that could very well render her unconscious, but Elaine could not deny the profound sense of dread nestling in the pit of her stomach.

Henry took a step back and gazed into the thicketed wilderness they had just come from. With a nod, Henry gestured towards the jungle and said, "In there."

Chapter 14

Louisa cried out with fear and then clamped her hand over her mouth at the sight of a coiling black snake. With her back against the tree trunk, Louisa set her hands on the ground to regain some sense of balance. As the serpent slithered closer, Louisa's bright blue eyes widened with fear. She felt paralyzed in a sense, falling prey to the snake's charm.

But then Louisa snapped out of her lucid state and got to her feet, running with every ounce of energy left in her. There were hanging vines and slimy creatures all about, while Louisa scanned the jungle sky overhead. Despite her terror, she could not deny that the landscape before her was beautiful. Dangerous, but beautiful.

Just like William.

By the time Louisa reached the waterfall, she hunched over and clutched her knees to catch her breath. The flowing falls fed a blue lagoon, whose clear fresh water longed to be drank. Dying of thirst, Louisa knelt down and cupped her hand in the water, bringing the liquid to her lips. It tasted cool and wonderful. She was automatically at ease.

Louisa found comfort in listening to the waterfall, so she let the natural sounds of the jungle lull her to sleep as she slowly lay down to rest her head. She only intended to close her eyes for a moment, in the hope of calming her spirit. But sleep came instead.

* * *

When Louisa woke up hours later, daylight was gone and rain had replaced it. Looking down at her soiled dress, Louisa lifted her head to the sky and shielded her face with her arm. Lightning and thunder struck and boomed throughout the jungle, shaking the ground and illuminating the sky.

Louisa sat up on her knees and looked around in all directions. Her clothes and hair were soaked, and she was already shivering from the cold. Her teeth chattered as she rubbed her hands over her arms to warm herself. When a lightning bolt struck straight ahead, Louisa rose to her feet and stared ahead at the glorious magnificence of it.

Another bolt of lightning descended from the black sky up above and struck a tree that rivalled the height of the tallest buildings in New York. Louisa heard an indescribable crack and lifted her head to spot the noise. As her blue eyes raced to the top of the tree, it split at the base and tipped over. Screeching at the sight, Louisa grabbed the skirt of her dress and took off, sprinting as if she were being chased by a pack of wolves.

As her feet pounded against the slick forest floor, Louisa looked back over her shoulder at the descending tree. But then she skidded against the wet grass and collapsed face first onto the ground. With no mercy, the tree gave way like a crashing wave and Louisa screamed.

Just before the tree landed on Louisa, someone leapt forward and snatched Louisa out of the way. The tree collapsed to the ground with a violent thud as Louisa gasped at the close distance, for she was no more than a few footsteps away.

"Are you mad?" Frederic barked over the thunder, lying on top of her.

Louisa gazed up into his gray eyes, the cloudy irises she had once feared.

"What are you doing running about in the middle of a storm?" he scolded.

In a state of shock, Louisa swallowed and looked up at him with tears in her eyes.

Frederic shook his head in disappointment and stood up. Then he threaded his fingers through his long auburn locks and wiped the moisture from his face. When Louisa's eyes found his, Frederic extended an open hand and she took it, effortlessly rising to her feet.

"Thank you, sir." Louisa parted her lips and admired him as lightning flashed all around them. The storm picked up, progressing into a full-on downpour characterized by rain that shot sideways and came tumbling down in thick sheets. Louisa shivered.

"Come with me, girl." Frederic turned on his heel and traipsed through the jungle. Her small hand remained in his large one, as Frederic absentmindedly braided his fingers through hers. Louisa kept quiet and followed closely behind, still shaking like a leaf.

Frederic kept his eyes peeled, searching the woods for any potential threat. There was a dagger strapped to his belt, in case he should need to protect either of them. When he reached the makeshift shelter he had fashioned from palm fronds and tree limbs, Frederic steered her body into the small hut and crouched down beside her.

Leaning into the back of the shelter, Louisa pulled her knees into her chest and looked out at the pouring rain before them. She was thankful for the covering over her head, even though it hardly compared to a proper roof. Frederic removed a handkerchief from his pocket and swiped the cloth over his face and neck in effort to clean the dirt, grime, and sweat of the jungle away.

Louisa watched Frederic with a pair of careful, innocent eyes when he opened a flask of whiskey and took a long pull. After screwing the cap back on, Frederic dragged the back of his hand across his mouth and inched farther underneath the shelter. Their shoulders brushed and Frederic lowered his gaze, while Louisa's skin flushed at the brief contact.

"Louisa," he crooned, looking up to meet those pretty blue eyes. "What on earth were you thinking? Do you realize how easily you could have been killed?"

"You act as though I chose to be here," Louisa muttered. "But I was never given a choice." She held his gaze without blinking. "I am here because you kidnapped me."

Frederic clenched his jaw but could not look away.

"Correct me if I am wrong," Louisa declared, firmly looking him in the eye.

Frederic turned his head and watched the rain. "I never wanted to take you. You have no reason to believe me, but it is the truth."

"Then why did you?" Louisa countered, grabbing his shoulder. "Why did you take me?"

Frederic rubbed his lips together and sighed. When he glanced back at Louisa, her face was a portrait of young beauty. What he had done to her ripped his heart in two.

Unable to search those desperate blue eyes, Frederic stared at the ground and gritted his teeth together. "He has my father," he painfully confessed. "I am to do as Judas says for one year, in exchange for my father's freedom."

Anger fled Louisa immediately, as her face fell in realization and surprise.

"I am sorry for taking you," Frederic lamented. "Truly, I am."

Louisa hung her head and flinched when thunder boomed aloud.

"But you must understand that I had no choice." Frederic crawled out from under the shelter and walked straight into the storm, alarming Louisa. She clutched the skirt of her gown and followed the stranger, unable to describe why she felt close to him already.

"Frederic!" Louisa ran through the rain until she reached him. At the sound of her voice, Frederic froze in his tracks. "You'll be killed," Louisa cried, squeezing his arm.

When Frederic gazed upon her face, the expression on his own was emotionless. "Perhaps it is what I deserve," he mused. Plagued by guilt, Frederic pushed onward and Louisa's arm fell to her side.

"You saved my life," Louisa called after him. "I would be dead if it weren't for you."

"No." Frederic spun around and stalked towards her. "You are here because of me. You should be at home in New York. In that pretty little mansion by the sea."

"How could I go back now?" Louisa countered, taking a step closer.

Frederic cocked his head to the side but made a point to listen.

"My mother and father are dead. I have nothing in New York now," she said. "As if I could ever make it off this island." Louisa shook her head. "The only family I have left is trapped here with me, and I have no way of finding either of them."

A tear slid down Louisa's cheek as her lower lip trembled with fear.

Wanting to comfort her for all the pain he had caused, Frederic reached out to touch her. "Do not cry, dear Louisa." He swept the tear away with his thumb and set his hand on her shoulder. "I shall help you find your family. I promise."

Louisa sniffled, enjoying his gentle touch. "Really?"

Frederic placed his hand over his heart. "On my father's life."

Despite her tears, Louisa looked over his handsome face and smiled.

"Well, what have we here?" Judas raised his pistol and fired.

The moment Louisa screamed, Frederic clamped his hand around her wrist and they took off running. One shot fired after the next as the couple raced deeper and deeper into the jungle, Frederic tugging at Louisa's arm to propel her forward faster. Louisa tried not to make a sound, but it proved increasingly difficult for her to keep from crying out.

When Frederic spotted a robust tree with plenty of coverage overhead, he darted for the trunk and then gave Louisa a boost. She was frantic and shaking, so he had to push her hard before Louisa took the hint and placed her foot on the first branch. Then Frederic leapt up and climbed after her, taking her hand as he found a way to the top of the tree.

Camouflaged behind a vast supply of green leaves, Frederic crouched down on a stout limb, wide enough for the two of them to fit. Louisa trembled with fear at the pop of another gunshot, as her breath caught at the back of her throat. Frederic held her back to his chest and covered her mouth with his hand. "Be quiet," he whispered.

Tears rolled down Louisa's cheeks as Judas came into view on the ground below. He took a swig from the rum bottle in his hand and then aimed the pistol at the sky and fired. Louisa's shoulders shook, but Frederic wrapped his arm around her stomach to hold her still.

"Oh darling..." Judas called out, slurring his words. "Where are you, my love? Where are you, sweet Louisa?" Judas staggered forward and nearly fell on his face.

Louisa breathed through her nose and placed her hand over the one Frederic held over her mouth. It was the only comfort she had, and Louisa needed something to cling to.

"Louisa! It is William, my love! Your fiancé! Where are you?" he growled.

Louisa shut her eyes tight and relied on what breath she had left in her lungs.

"You cannot hide, my darling. You cannot hide from me!" Judas stalked forward, getting dangerously close to the ground beneath Frederic and Louisa. "I will find you."

Judas collapsed to the forest floor and fell into a state of unconsciousness.

Unable to believe their good fortune, Louisa watched Judas down below, the man she had once called William, the man she had once believed to be Captain of La Fleur Noire, the man she had once loved. But of one thing she was absolutely sure: none of it was true anymore.

"We must go, Louisa," Frederic whispered in her ear. "You do not want to be here when he wakes up." When she nodded, Frederic released her and leaned back.

Careful to keep quiet, Frederic made his slow descent down the mountainous tree. He held a hand out for Louisa to take as she climbed after him, worried her feet would hit the slick bark and send her flying to the hard ground. Frederic landed first and immediately turned back to pick Louisa up in his arms and then set her down on her own two feet.

Louisa looked over at Judas on the ground and a chill crept up her spine. But then Frederic grabbed her arm and steered her away from the villain. How could Louisa ever have loved someone as heinous as Judas? He wasn't William. Not anymore.

He was the devil.

Chapter 15

Henry and Elaine trekked through the jungle in the rain, disappointed that they had yet to find Louisa in the dark. Exhausted from their time at sea, the two found shelter beneath a gathering of trees, whose extended limbs and robust vegetation formed a canopy over their heads. Henry took a seat on the wet forest floor and watched Elaine settle down beside him, shivering from the prolonged storm.

"Let me see your face." Elaine reached out and touched Henry's cheek as he winced in pain. "Sorry." She pulled back, worried that she had hurt him.

"It is all right, my love," Henry replied with a smile. She could not understand his optimism until he explained, "I am just happy to be alive."

Elaine tucked a dark lock behind his ear, admiring the way he looked in the night. "I like your hair longer," she said, curling her finger through a strand.

Henry gazed into her eyes and uttered, "I like yours longer as well."

When Elaine dropped her hand from his face, Henry took it and squeezed.

"Where is she, Henry? How are we ever going to find her?" Elaine averted her gaze, but Henry kept his eyes on those green gems.

"You know this island better than anyone else," Henry noted. "You lived here for years. If anyone can find Louisa, it is you, Elaine."

Failing to share his confidence, Elaine hung her head in distress and Henry stroked her jawline in comfort. "What have they done with her?" Elaine feared, recalling the look of terror in Louisa's eyes when that man took her away.

"Listen to me." Henry held Elaine's face in his hands. "We will find her. So help me God, we will." His golden eyes were warm, yet determined. He meant what he said.

Elaine nodded and buried her face in Henry's chest. Henry wrapped his arms around Elaine and held her close, as they clung to each other in the night. The way he figured it, they had lived on the island before and survived. Why would anything be different the second time around? If anything, they had an advantage that no one else did.

"I'm going to kill him," Elaine mumbled into Henry's shirt.

Henry leaned back so he could look into her eyes. "What?"

"I'm going to kill him," she repeated. "I've

done it once. I'll do it again."

Henry pondered in silence for a moment, though his eyes never left hers. Eventually, he said, "If you don't, I will."

Elaine returned her head to Henry's chest and listened to his heartbeat. "What have they done to her, Henry? What do they plan to do?"

"We will find her, Elaine," Henry chanted. "We will find her."

Elaine wrapped her arms around Henry's rib cage and squeezed tight. "I miss her," she whimpered, a silent tear running down from her eye. "I miss Lilly. I miss our baby."

Henry rubbed her back and consoled her quietly. "I know. I miss her, too."

Henry held Elaine as she cried, wishing to get her off this godforsaken island. In all his life, Henry had never imagined that they would be forced to return. Yet to Elaine, the place must have somehow felt like home. Could that be her only ray of light in the dark?

"You will see her again, darling," Henry whispered. "I promise."

Elaine touched her cheek to the warmth of Henry's neck and crawled into his lap. Stroking his fingers through her hair, Henry placed his other hand at the small of her back and sighed. When he first met Elaine on the island, Henry could have sworn that she was no more than a child. Sixteen, perhaps. The age of Louisa now.

"Did you see it?" Elaine asked, interrupting his

thoughts.

"Yes," he acknowledged. "I have seen it."

"Makes me think of Jade," Elaine wept, curling her body into Henry and praying that he would never have to let go.

When the ship first arrived, Henry and Elaine had both spotted the vacant place onshore where the shack used to be. It had been their home. The place where they fought. The place where they loved. The only reason Lilly had been born.

But now it was all gone, no more than a distant memory. Any shred of the life they had shared on the island burned to pieces that night in the fire. And everything about the island they had once known, the island they had just lost, made them think of Jade.

Lost in a memory, Elaine lowered her gaze and recalled the baby panther in her arms on the night of her father's murder. She had quivered and hissed, while Elaine held her back and hid behind a gathering of palm fronds. Years later, Elaine never could have imagined that the same monster would return to slay Jade.

Her vibrant green eyes came to mind, along with her sleek black fur coat. Elaine stared off into the jungle, wishing for her feline friend to appear in the thunderstorm and come to her rescue. If only Elaine could have saved Jade, protected her from Judas in the same way Jade had intervened just in time. Had Elaine been left alone in the jungle with Judas a moment longer, she would surely be dead and Lilly never would have been given a chance.

Henry sat in silence with a haunted look on his face. Recognizing the gleam in his eyes, Elaine turned her focus on him and rested her palm against his chest. "What is it, Henry?" She circled her hand over his shirt and asked, "What are you thinking about?"

He looked at her and inhaled. "Murder."

Chapter 16

As the sun emerged with a new day, Louisa awoke curled up in Frederic's arms. With her eyelids fluttering, Louisa nuzzled his neck and soaked up his warmth. He smelled so wonderful and masculine, which she found highly appealing. Perhaps he had been her kidnapper. But today, he was the man who had saved her life.

Just as Louisa dozed back off, Frederic touched her hair and lowered his lips to her ear. "Stay as you are."

Bristling with fear, Louisa gazed up at Frederic as he tightened his arm around her and looked over her shoulder. There was pure fear in his murky gray eyes, and it made Louisa's heart race. Especially when a grunting creature stomped the ground behind them.

Frederic clenched his jaw and stared directly at the beast, unwilling to be made a coward. The wild animal flicked his dark dirty ears and failed to blink.

Louisa heard thrumming in her ears as she watched Frederic and clung to the collar of his shirt. His palm pressed into the small of her back, and she tensed at the urgency of his contact. It must have meant that danger, or even death, was undoubtedly near.

"Don't move," Frederic whispered.

Louisa closed her eyes and stayed down. The beast stomped his foot against the ground and charged. Relying on instinct alone, Frederic reared back and threw a stout butcher knife that landed along the creature's neck. It was a clean cut, but a deadly one, indeed.

With a successfully sliced artery, the beast had no choice but to topple over and bleed out. When the creature hit the ground, Louisa flinched at the thud. She looked to Frederic for reassurance, as he stared straight ahead and rose to his feet.

"What was that?" Louisa panted, catching her breath.

"Wild boar." Frederic strode towards the beast and removed the knife. As he wiped the blood away, Louisa sat up and leaned forward on her knees to study him.

"How did you do that?" She felt an equal amount of gratitude and fear for the speed with which he had slaughtered the beast. If he could slaughter a wild boar with such precision and ease, then what was he capable of doing to her?

"Do what?" Frederic returned the blade to its sheath and concealed it beneath his clothing.

"Kill that creature so effortlessly," Louisa replied, still wholly stunned.

"I am a hunter, Louisa. It is what I do." He knelt down before the dead beast and searched its glassy eyes for any sign of life.

"A hunter?" Louisa echoed, her voice catching at the back of her throat.

"Yes," Frederic hissed. "A very good one, too. Why do you think he chose me? The only reason he has kept my father alive."

"You know these woods," Louisa assumed, turning her head to regard them.

"Not these woods," he corrected her. "Any woods."

"That is an awfully bold statement coming from—"

"The man who just saved your life," he finished for her. A sly smirk came across his face as he glared across the way. After all, him rescuing the girl had become a routine gesture as of late. "Spare me the lecture on vanity, child. I haven't the time for it."

"Child?" Louisa started. "I'm not a child."

"How old are you then?" he challenged, holding her gaze.

"Sixteen." Louisa held her head high and crossed her arms over her chest.

"Who is the proud one now?" Frederic countered, brushing her arm as he walked past her. She was a child, but the man in him viewed young Louisa as much more than that.

"Frederic," she called, turning on her heel and chasing after him. "Where are you going?" She had no reason to follow him, other than the sheer fact that she wanted to.

Frederic wiped the sleeve of his shirt against his forehead to collect the sweat that had gathered there. "We must move deeper into the forest. With Judas and those wild creatures on the loose, it is simply not safe."

"But what about my brother? What about Henry and Elaine?" Louisa reached out and grabbed his arm. "They are family, and you promised that you would help me find them."

"And I will, Louisa," Frederic acknowledged. "But not today."

Louisa let go of Frederic's arm as he straightened his shoulders and kept walking. He was a proud, tall man, clearly accustomed to calling the shots. Perhaps a little defiance would do him good.

"I'm not going with you," Louisa declared, planting her feet firmly on the ground.

Frederic froze and turned around to look back at her.

"You heard me," she clarified. "I'm not going with you, Frederic."

He took one step towards her and then another until their faces were only inches apart. "Yes, you are."

"No, I'm not," Louisa rebelled. She lifted her head and glowered into his gray eyes. "And you can't make me."

Frederic grabbed her arm and jerked her in front of him while she bucked and flailed about like a wild horse. If she had known better, Louisa would have heeded the protection of a strong man on a treacherous island such as this. She was certainly going to need it.

"I'll scream," Louisa threatened, jabbing her finger in his direction.

"A lot of good that would do you." Frederic tightened his hold on her arm and squeezed. "Would you like to be walking around one night and have Judas come up on you instead?"

"No," Louisa scowled, gritting her teeth. Frederic tugged at her arm and dragged her after him, even though she could barely keep up. "Let go of me!" Louisa slapped his chest, and when he released her she stumbled to the ground.

With her hands in the dirt, Louisa got on her knees and forced herself to stand. She caught her breath and regarded authoritative Frederic, whose chest was rising and falling just the same. Louisa wiped her palms on her dress and gazed up at him once he spoke.

"You are foolish." Frederic stood beside her and levelled his eyes in disappointment. "A foolish, silly girl." His eyes raced over her face, because he longed for her to stay.

Louisa fluttered her lashes and looked down, feeling his searching gaze on her. When she was brave enough to respond, Louisa glanced up and said, "I'm going to find my brother and his wife. And you're not going to stop me." She looked deep into his eyes with every word, pressing the resilience of her declaration onto him with great force.

Frederic flared his nostrils and looked over her pretty face one last time. It was an innocent face distinguished by beauty and youth. But what if he never saw it again?

As Louisa turned on her heel to head back the way they came, Frederic grabbed her arm. "Wait," he said, desperate for just a little more time with her. Frederic reached into the pocket of his pants and handed her a small knife. "Take this."

Louisa took the blade from his large palm but was careful not to let her fingers touch his skin. Although the weapon would be difficult to hunt with, the knife could serve as a successful deterrent, in case she needed to slice the throat of an enemy. Without Frederic's protection, the blade was better than nothing.

"Thank you," Louisa uttered, taking a step back to lengthen the distance between them.

"Be careful," was all Frederic had to say before the moment was gone.

And then Louisa went her way and Frederic went his.

Chapter 17

Henry batted through the branches in his way as he and Elaine plowed their way through the jungle. It was high noon, and with only a handful of nuts and berries to munch on, Henry and Elaine were famished. Every attempt to find Louisa had proved unsuccessful, while Judas was nowhere to be found.

"I need to rest." Henry sat down at the base of a tree and swept his stringy dark hair from his forehead. Every lock was soaked with sweat, and Henry thought that he might die of thirst. Only a mouthful of cool liquid from the lagoon, and he would be content.

"Stay here." Elaine leaned down to touch Henry's shoulder. "I'll fetch us water."

Henry nodded and brushed his thumb across his upper lip. Before she could take off, Henry clasped Elaine's elbow and left a gentle kiss on her mouth. When she stood up, Elaine smiled down at her husband, already in a hurry to come back to him.

She took careful, calculated steps on her way to the lagoon. Once she reached the clear pool of water, Elaine knelt down and covered her face with the liquid. Then she drank as much water as she could, slurping it down by the handful.

For a moment, Elaine sat back and watched the waterfall, taking delight in the spectacle of Mother Nature's beautiful creation. The sound was like music to her ears. It made her think of her childhood. It made her think of her father. It made her think of Jade.

Tired of reminiscing over a past that had no capacity to change, Elaine filled two coconut halves with water for Henry. They had knocked them down from a beach tree at daybreak with a pair of rocks. While poor sustenance would hold them over for now, Elaine knew they would need to fish soon. Nuts and berries could only last so long.

On her journey back, Elaine recalled the very first time she had laid eyes on Henry. Their meeting had not been a conventional one, but a memory that was forever burned into her brain. The way they had fallen in love held a similar claim over her heart.

When Elaine returned to the spot where she had left Henry, he had seamlessly disappeared. Taking a shallow breath, Elaine spun in a slow circle and searched all around the forest. But Henry was gone.

Her green eyes dilated and widened, as she took a few careful steps forward. A branch wobbled nearby, compelling Elaine to whip her head around and stare into the beady black eyes of a watchful bird. Her shoulders sagged in relief when the creature chirped a delightful tune, but the bird had no answer to her question. Where was Henry?

Shaking the matter off, Elaine pressed onward though refrained from making a sound. They had enemies in this jungle, and the last thing she wanted to do was alert them.

But then Elaine spotted a fresh trail of blood at her feet and stopped in her tracks. The crimson liquid forged a thin path before her. One that she would rather die than not take.

Elaine dropped the coconut halves as the water they had held splashed across her feet. Loud blood throbbed in her ears, hot and angry. She swallowed and took off running, plowing her way through the jungle as she followed the trail of blood.

Tears stung Elaine's eyes, because she knew that something was wrong. She could hardly think or breathe, her heart pounding with a vengeance. But then the trail of blood came to an abrupt end, and Elaine found Henry on the other side of it.

Her stomach dropped and the edges of her vision clouded into a painful blur. Judas had a pistol in his hand, and the end of the weapon was pressed against Henry's temple.

"You think you can outsmart me?" Judas barked, his arm wrapped tightly beneath Henry's chest. There was blood all over Henry's clothing, and it terrified Elaine to think of where it must have been coming from.

Elaine took a cautious step forward and held her breath, wondering how to remedy the situation while keeping Henry's life intact. He could barely keep his eyes open, his knees buckling in defeat. Elaine realized that he hardly had any strength left.

"You think I don't see you?" Judas demanded, angry and shouting. Birds scattered at the booming sound of his voice. "You think I'm not watching you, island girl?"

Feeling brazen, Elaine rushed towards him until he turned the pistol on her. Forced to stay still, Elaine held her hands in the air and searched his cobalt eyes. "I'll do whatever you want, Judas," she declared. "Just let him go."

Judas relaxed his grip on the gun and let the weapon dangle at his side. "You've said that before," he reminded her. "But you broke the terms of our agreement."

"So did you," Elaine fired back. "You promised that no harm would come to my family. To Louisa or Henry." She nodded her head towards her husband. "You lied."

Judas smiled and Elaine felt a chill creep down her spine at the sight. Then he raised the pistol and aimed it directly at her face. "Well then," he sneered, aggressive and vicious. "Perhaps I'll start with you."

"No," Henry protested, coughing and gagging. He clenched his jaw and spit, but all Elaine saw was blood. "Take me."

"What?" Elaine felt frozen, as if a block of quicksand had formed around her feet. "NO!"

"I suppose that will do," Judas replied. "The girl is the only one I need anyway." He nodded towards Elaine and winked.

"NO!" Elaine shouted. "You can't kill Henry! I won't let you!"

"Really, island girl?" Judas cocked the pistol and pointed it at her again. "How?"

Elaine gritted her teeth and balled her hands into fists at her sides. Then, when she was least expecting it, Judas put the pistol to Henry's head and fired.

"NOOOOO!" Elaine screamed, falling to her knees.

But Henry remained standing on both feet, as the sound of gunfire failed to echo throughout the jungle. Even though Judas had pulled the trigger, no bullet came out. The pistol was empty.

Finding humor in the matter, Judas tossed the pistol aside and stared at Elaine. She placed her hand over her heart and watched the rise and fall of Henry's chest. If Judas had killed him, Elaine felt sure her heart would have stopped.

Before Elaine could fully appreciate the fact that Henry was still alive, Judas grabbed him by the collar and dragged him to the edge of an approaching cliff. It was a break in the island, where a small river ran between two tall pieces of land. Caught off guard, Elaine panicked and could hardly get the words out of the back of her throat.

"Judas, don't!" she cried. "Please!"

But Judas had never been a man of mercy.

"HENRY!"

Judas pushed Henry off the cliff, and he fell forward without the slightest of difficulty. Consumed with rage, Elaine snatched the empty pistol off the ground and bashed it into Judas's skull. His eyes rolled back into his head as he crumpled to the ground.

Panting loudly, Elaine knelt down and leaned over the edge of the cliff, but Henry was nowhere to be found. She missed his landing and could not be sure if the river had caught him. If it had, Henry could be floating downstream or climbing onto the bank. But if it had not, then Henry would surely be dead.

Elaine turned back to find Judas knocked out cold. She would have killed him if there had been bullets in the gun. But since there were none, Elaine grabbed the empty pistol and hurried off into the forest.

She had to find Henry.

Chapter 18

Alone in the jungle, Louisa felt a shift in temperature when the air turned cool at nightfall. She wrapped her arms around her body out of a need for comfort rather than warmth. With Frederic, she had felt undoubtedly safe. It wasn't until now, when he was gone, that Louisa realized separating from him had been a grave mistake.

To her absolute and utter disappointment, Louisa had failed to stumble upon Henry or Elaine today in the jungle. Perhaps that had been the reason why Frederic insisted they wait to search for them. On her own, Louisa's attempt had been fruitless. She was probably walking in circles at this point, because the past three hours had amounted to as much.

Louisa was damp with sweat, and the moisture made her clothing stick to her skin like glue. She was anxious and uncomfortable, willing to trade anything in exchange for a hot bath. As she trudged on in the wilderness, Louisa thought to seek out the waterfall. Surely, she could freshen up at the lagoon and quench her dying thirst.

But Louisa had never learned her way around the jungle, solely relying on Frederic as her guide. What a fool she had been to send him away at a time like this. Though Louisa would never own up to it, she needed him now.

Transfixed by the rising moon up above, Louisa failed to watch where she was walking and tripped, crying out. She tumbled and rolled down a hill, hearing the fabric of her dress rip against a tree root. Startled and alert, Louisa reached the hard ground and gasped aloud, biting her tongue to cope with the pain.

Her back ached and a bloody gash had already formed across the face of her knee. If only she had been more careful, rather than fumbling about the jungle in the night. Louisa winced in pain and lifted her head to observe the steep drop off she had tumbled down. How she had been blind enough to never see it, she did not know.

As Louisa got to her feet, she brushed her palms off on her dress and regained her balance. Trudging forward, she reached out and grabbed ahold of a tree branch to steady herself. But her brow furrowed in discomfort when she noticed the murky swamp before her. However was she going to get out of this mess?

"Help..."

Louisa stilled at the sound of a man's voice,

her skin prickling with fear.

"Help me. Please," he croaked.

Holding on to the skirting of her gown, Louisa walked along the edge of the swamp until she discovered Judas on the ground, covered in his own blood. Since he was defenseless, Louisa knelt down before him and placed her hand to his chest. There was a cut across his forehead and a thicker red substance in his hair which must have been blood. The contrast against his pale blonde hair left the blood illuminated by the moonlight.

"Louisa, please. Help me," he begged, reaching out for her hand.

Swallowing, Louisa paused for a moment to reflect on her stupidity. Why had she come to him and how could she have any empathy for the scoundrel? But he was vulnerable and hurt, incapable of harming her anymore. Perhaps now was the best time to forgive his trespasses and show Judas compassion. After all, she had loved him just months ago.

"What happened?" Louisa let him take her small hand in his, even when he squeezed too tight. The gesture should have been a warning that he had more strength than he let on. But Louisa wanted him to be good, the way he had once been, for a change. She wanted to believe that for just one night, Judas could be her William.

"A beast in the wild," he explained, hissing as he took the next breath.

"A wild boar?" She looked over him with

concern. There was an awful lot of blood, though she could not name the source. But she had seen the wild boar with her very eyes, and it would have slaughtered her had it not been for Frederic. So she believed him.

Judas nodded while wincing in pain. "It attacked me," he rasped

Louisa looked off to the side and tried to get ahold of herself. What was the wisest course of action to take? How could she protect herself and do the right thing?

"How can you ever expect me to help you?" she demanded, digging her nails into his flesh when he squeezed her hand harder. "After all the horrible things you have done?"

"Oh, Louisa." Judas touched her cheek, absentmindedly smearing blood across her face. "My dear, sweet Louisa." His voice was like a cooling elixir on a sore, open wound.

"You lied to me," she accused, shaking her head in disgust. Despite those dreadful months at sea, it would take time for her to accept the fact that their engagement had been nothing more than a ruse. "You kidnapped me. And then, last night... well you—"

"I was drunk, Louisa," he defended. "Have you no compassion for my weaknesses? You were always the greatest of them all."

As he stroked a bloody finger through her hair, Louisa flinched. The stench of his breath made her cover her mouth with her hand. Judas was not the William she had known in New York. So why did she want him to be so badly?

"Did you ever truly love me?" Louisa wondered. "Did you ever care for me at all?"

"You know I did, my love." Judas rubbed his thumb along her jawline and down her neck, spreading his blood everywhere. "I still care about you. Even now."

"Then why have you done all of this?" Louisa gestured her hand in the air. She wanted an apology, and all he had were excuses. Some groveling was to be expected.

Judas took her face in his hands, a pair of blue eyes staring into another. "There is darkness within me, and I can't stop it. I've tried, but..." Judas shook his head, looking off.

"Well you must try harder, my darling." Louisa bit her tongue, but the term of affection had slipped so loosely from her mouth. At least Judas was admitting his faults.

"Do you still love me, Louisa?" Judas rubbed his bloody palms over her arms before cupping her waist. Surely her dress was utterly ruined, covered with crimson stains.

Louisa wanted to look away but those cobalt irises kept her eyes clearly focused on him, like he possessed the spirit of a snake charmer. Judas touched her back and pulled her into his lap, covering her mouth with a bruising kiss. When the emotion he ignited within her became too much, Louisa grabbed his arms and pulled away.

"Yes, I still love you," Louisa cried. "Is that what you want to hear?"

Thunder rumbled overhead as heavy rain came down in sheets. Judas ran his thumb beneath Louisa's mouth until her lips parted for him. Back in New York, he had touched her mind in ways that no future man would ever be able to understand.

"We can still be together," Judas proposed, tugging at her heartstrings and what affection she had left. "I have thought everything through. I have a plan."

"No." Louisa peeled his hands from her face. "I cannot trust you anymore."

"Why, darling," Judas sympathized, wrapping his fingers over her shoulders. "Of course you can." He set those cobalt irises on her and stared into her eyes until she looked away.

Louisa lowered her head and wept, so Judas took the opportunity to pull her in close. As he held her, precarious thoughts raced across Louisa's mind. If he truly was bad, then wouldn't he have done something to harm her by now? Perhaps the absence of his malevolence was a true testament to the fact that he had changed, that he was different now. Was it wrong of her to hope for that? To dream of William Pierce again?

"If you love me, then we can be together again," Judas coaxed, tucking her head beneath his chin. He squeezed her tight and said, "I can make all the pain go away."

Grappling with indecision, Louisa dug her nails into his shirt, hoping they would pierce his flesh. She felt so helpless and confused, alone in the jungle with no one but Judas for guidance and comfort. What should she do? Believe him? Or run?

Either option came with a risk. There was no ensuring her freedom now.

When a bolt of lightning struck nearby, the noise startled Louisa until she began coughing. Judas immediately patted her on the back and then handed her a tall glass bottle.

"Here," Judas urged, rubbing her arm. "Drink this." When Louisa cast a weary glance in his direction, Judas looked down at her with a smile. "It's just water," he said.

Fighting the lump in her throat, Louisa looked into his beautiful eyes and could have sworn that she saw trust there. Or perhaps that was just a reflection of the love in her own.

Wanting to make her wish come true, Louisa grabbed the bottle and pressed the rim to her lips. The glass felt cool against the palm of her hand, but as she sucked down the water it had a bitter taste. Heat rushed over her skin, because she had taken a drink from the devil.

"There now, Louisa." Judas took the bottle from her and set it on the ground. Then he patted her on the back and curled his fingers through her hair. "All better."

Louisa turned her head from left to right,

though it seemed to take her a year to do so. Blinking became a heavy burden, as she tried to recall what she was doing. There was a sudden tingling in her fingertips followed by an incessant ringing in her ears. Louisa held her hand to her head and peered out, but everything was turning blurry.

"You look well, my darling," Judas crooned. "Very well, indeed."

Louisa could hardly grasp the sound of his voice, for it sounded light years away. Before she opened her mouth to speak, all the thoughts seemed to drift away. She leaned down on her side and put her cheek against the ground, closing her eyes so she could sleep.

Chapter 19

By the time Louisa flickered her eyes awake, the world was already a dull blur around her. "William?" she called, helplessly disoriented. "William?"

"Yes, my darling." Judas was crouched down before her, doting and patient.

"Am I dreaming?" She felt stuck to the ground like cement, but couldn't understand the feeling. Thunder boomed and lightning struck in the distance, though she didn't flinch.

"Yes, my love." Judas touched her cheek and smiled.

"What is happening to me?" Louisa felt bound, restrained, incapable of movement. Yet she lacked the capacity to understand why. Had it all been a bad dream?

"You are crossing over to the other side," Judas revealed confidently.

"The other side?" She sounded sleepy and incoherent, for she could hardly remember her own name. "The other side of what?"

Before she could breathe, Judas turned Louisa's hands over and sliced her palms with a blade. Her breath caught at the back of her throat as she cried out in pain, hardly able to believe what he had done to her. Tears streamed down her cheeks, but Judas didn't care.

Instead, he took her hands and rubbed them all over her dress, covering the fabric in her blood. At that very moment, Louisa looked around long enough to figure out why she couldn't move. During her hypnotic slumber, Judas had tied her to a tree.

Realizing the fault in her actions, Louisa cringed with emotion, but there was no undoing her mistake. "HELP!" she shouted, praying that someone would be lurking nearby and hear her. "HELP!" She was frantic and shaking. "ELAINE! HENRY!"

Judas covered her mouth with a dirty hand before she could yell for Frederic. "You won't speak a word!" Judas hissed. "Do you understand me?"

Every cry came out muffled, as Louisa screamed in terror. But Judas was alive with bloodlust, the crimson substance across his clothing clearly not his own. He had fooled her. He had tricked her. He had hoodwinked her. Again.

Louisa sobbed and kicked her legs back and forth, but her feeble attempt at breaking free was no match for Judas. He sat down on her calves and pinned her arms to her side, stringing more rope around her body and fastening it to the tree. Once he had her tied up, Judas stuffed a handkerchief into her mouth so no one could hear her scream. His faux initials were embroidered into the cloth in baby blue cursive. How deceptive.

Unwilling to succumb, Louisa bucked and flailed about, struggling to break free.

Judas pressed his hand down on her thighs until she was forced to lay her legs flat. Then he grabbed her chin and kissed her. "You were always a beautiful girl. Yet so naïve."

Steaming red blood pulsed through her veins like fire.

"Your father is dead. Your mother is dead. And now Henry."

Louisa stared at Judas as all of the breath left her lungs. The handkerchief was slowly creeping to the back of her throat, but she didn't care if she choked on it. Henry was gone.

"I killed him, Louisa," Judas confessed. "He was so pathetic and weak."

Louisa groaned and Judas clamped his hand around her arm. She whimpered at the bruising grip, in as much physical pain as she was emotional. Her loving, caring, protective older brother was gone, and there was no hope of her ever seeing him again.

"Now I have that pretty little wife of his all to myself." Judas pressed the tip of the dagger against

Louisa's cheek, though not enough to draw blood. "First Henry, then you." His breath raced down her neck and she shivered. "She was all I ever wanted anyway."

Louisa shut her eyes tight in the hope that it would make this all go away. But then Judas placed the blade to her neck, and her eyes were wide open. She cried out, but the plea was continuously muffled. No one was going to hear her.

"Goodbye, my love." Judas left a rough kiss on her forehead and stood up. "You'll make a lovely bride in heaven."

Judas placed the blade in his pocket and scurried off, disappearing into the forest. As he walked away and left Louisa to die, Judas felt proud of himself for taking care of brother and sister in one day. What an accomplishment.

As Louisa sat there awaiting death, she tried to spit the handkerchief out of her mouth, but it was caught near her throat. Every ounce of hope left her soul, while every bit of dread replaced it. Just when matters couldn't get any worse, something swam towards her, rippling the waters of the still marshy swamp. It was a crocodile.

Louisa shrieked and cried out for help, shaking uncontrollably in horror. Once she recognized that her clothing and skin were covered in blood, it became all the more apparent why Judas had left her so. Louisa was live bait.

The crocodile surfaced from the swamp and

began crawling up the bank towards her. Louisa yelled in terror, taking in the sight of the beast. From where she sat, Louisa could make out the deadly, sinister nature of its teeth. She studied its eyes and saw nothing but pure evil. The sheer natural drive to kill. And eat.

As the beast picked up speed, Louisa shut her eyes and looked away. The only comfort she had was that she would see her mother, father, and brother again. Perhaps they would make a nice family in heaven.

Just before the crocodile reached Louisa, Frederic struck it across the head with a wooden plank. He beat the croc against the nose again and again, as the creature grew desperate to retrace its steps. Violently resilient, Frederic hit the animal with as much force as he could before it finally retreated into the swamp and quickly swam away.

Dropping the board, Frederic rushed over to Louisa and pulled the handkerchief out of her mouth. Crying and shaken, Louisa wept inconsolably as Frederic cut the ropes binding her body and freed her. But once she was unbound, Louisa was in such a state of shock that she sat there gazing straight ahead.

"Louisa, it is all right." Frederic touched her shoulder and she flinched. Biting his lip, he loathed Judas for what he had done to her. "It's Frederic. I am here."

Trembling in grief and fear, Louisa buried her face in her hands and mourned. She mourned the death of her parents. She mourned the death of Henry. She mourned the death of herself. Of the girl who believed in fairy tales and happy endings.

With a sigh of empathy, Frederic picked her up and carried her away in his arms. Careful not to alert anyone else in the jungle, Frederic took slow and deliberate steps until he reached the small shelter he had assembled throughout the day. When he set Louisa down, she felt cold to the touch. So he gave her some space and crawled underneath a series of branches and leaves, thankful the storm had let up. But Louisa pulled her knees into her chest and shivered, rocking back and forth, in a pure state of paranoia.

"Louisa," Frederic called, worried that she felt isolated and alone in the corner. "Louisa, you must say something."

"What would you like me to say?" she forced out despite her chattering teeth.

Frederic extended his hand to place on her back, then thought twice about it. "Anything."

"Judas left me for dead." Her voice cracked as she uttered, "And he killed my brother." Louisa broke down all over again, sobbing and shaking to the point that it must have been causing her physical pain. She was an absolute and utter mess, but still just as beautiful.

"What?" Frederic watched her and moved closer, touching the side of her shoulder.

Louisa turned to face Frederic for the first time and looked into his eyes. "Henry is dead," she revealed, weeping like a slaughtered animal. Tears and blood were everywhere.

Frederic rubbed the sleeve of Louisa's dress to provide some sense of comfort. Unbelievably broken, she sailed into his arms and rested her head on his chest. Unsure of what to do next, Frederic stroked his fingers through her hair and held her close. If Louisa wished, his shoulder was the only one she would ever need to cry on again.

While Louisa shuddered and wept, Frederic circled his palm over her back. His mind was churning with the perfectly plotted plan for revenge. A warranted search in the jungle.

He would find Judas.

And he would kill him.

Chapter 20

At the break of dawn, Elaine rose with the intent to find her husband. Last night had proved unsuccessful, as she traipsed about the jungle in the rainstorm. She had searched high and low for Henry, slipping along the wet grass and stumbling to her feet more times than not. There was even a shallow gash along her chin from fighting so hard.

When lightning struck, Elaine had sunk down to the hard ground on her knees and cried out loud. Tears streamed down her cheeks, because she could not accept the probable outcome of her one true love. No matter how dire the circumstances, she had to know whether or not he was alive.

If he had perished from the fall, Henry deserved a proper burial. He had been an honorable gentleman and the kindest man Elaine had ever known. She loved him with every fiber of her being, dead or alive. But what if the spare chance remained that Henry could be fighting for his life down below? That the fall had not killed Henry, but left him severely injured instead? That he had been crying out for Elaine all through the night, wondering why she could not hear him, wondering why she would not answer back?

Determined to find him, Elaine fashioned a walking stick from a stray branch that had fallen in the storm. Apart from Judas's empty pistol, it was her only weapon. But the stick could surely fend off any wild animals that might come prowling in the shadows of the forest.

For the better part of the morning, Elaine trudged through the jungle with pure adrenaline flooding her veins. She could not decide how to climb down to that low place, where Henry had fallen the day before. Though Elaine had revisited the scene of the incident, the cliff only extended so far. If only she could discover an area where either edge joined, forming a bridge over the river to the other side.

Elaine feathered her fingers through her black locks and sighed, pausing in her tracks. Even if she traveled to the other side, Henry would not be there. He had fallen into the pit down below, just as likely to have landed in the river as to have not.

Tired of debating the issue, Elaine looked over the edge and watched the stream of water flowing down below. She bit her lip and pondered, her green eyes darting from left to right at the sound of someone approaching. When the noise belonged to a lime colored frog bouncing from leaf to leaf, Elaine flared her nostrils and held her balance.

It was a steep drop to the ground below, nearly several hundred feet. But she parted her lips to release a breath of oxygen before inhaling deeply and swallowing. Without a moment to lose, she sat down on the cliff and let her legs dangle over the edge. Then she grabbed the walking stick and chucked it into the gaping hole, careful to hold on.

Leaning over for a peek, Elaine watched the stick crash against the ground and barely miss the river. If Henry had fallen in a similar manner, then his demise had been one of inevitability, not chance. But Elaine swallowed and clenched her teeth anyway.

Deep down, she knew the decision had already been made up in her mind. Even if Henry were already dead, she couldn't risk the chance of him actually being alive. What if he had pulled himself from the river and crawled off to protect himself during the storm? Henry could very well be nursing his wounds and starving to death for all she knew.

The truth was plain to see. The man Elaine loved might be surviving within a very limited window of time. How long the window might last, she did not know. But if Elaine did nothing, then he would die anyway, and she could not live with herself as long as the possibility existed. No, Elaine would find Henry, even if she died trying.

With one last breath, Elaine whispered a silent

prayer and shut her eyes. Then she grasped every bit of strength left inside of her and slowly eased herself off the edge. As her body turned in the opposite direction, Elaine grabbed the forest floor and tugged at a few blades of grass. When she looked down, her feet found a rock to rely upon and she began her slow descent down the side of the cliff.

After stepping from one stone to the next, Elaine placed a palm where each foot had just been, carefully plotting her next move. But the bottom of Elaine's foot had turned clammy with damp sweat. So when it connected with the next rock, her leg flew out from under her.

Elaine felt her hands begin to slip from their hold and cried out, looking up at the clifftop above. She had hardly scaled much of the incline, which indicated that if she fell, it would ultimately result in her death. When her legs began to tremble, Elaine's entire body quaked and she could not resist the dreadful feeling that it was over.

But then she spotted a hanging vine out of the corner of her eye and reached out to grab it. When she pulled and the vine failed to snap, Elaine wrapped two hands around the slimy green plant. Steadying her breathing, Elaine closed her eyes to keep herself from looking down. Then, when she was ready, Elaine clung tightly to the vine and walked her way down the cliff with the heels of her feet rubbing against the rock.

By some miracle, Elaine reached the bottom unscathed and dropped down to the ground with the vine in her hands. She sat there for a moment and caught her breath, lifting her head to observe the height of the cliff up above. Then Elaine rose to her feet and approached the river to wash her hands and cleanse her palate with a cooling drink.

Her hands shook as she smoothed the water through her hair until her black locks were slicked back. Elaine rested her palms on her thighs and stared into the rushing water, searching for her reflection in the river. At that moment, Elaine realized that the water must have been moving towards something, for flowing rivers always travel somewhere.

Curious, Elaine stood up and walked alongside the stream until her ears perked up. She recognized the sound of cascading waters and looking over once she reached the edge. Elaine hung her head in disappointment, for the river dropped off into a beautiful waterfall, far more intimidating in girth and height than the falls at the lagoon.

For a minute, Elaine stood there and gazed out at the exquisite view. She saw monkeys swinging from limb to limb as they played among the trees, running after one another. Colorful birds danced about the sky, practically pirouetting before the clouds, as if they were a pair of talented dancers and Elaine was their ticket to the stage.

Somehow, a smile forged its way across her

face because there was so much beauty in the wild. As she closed her eyes, a cool breeze drifted through Elaine's dark tresses, framing them in whimsical fashion around her face. Lost in the moment, she listened to Mother Nature's music and let her heart swell with joy. She certainly needed it.

When Elaine fluttered her lashes and looked out, a glorious rainbow hung over the jungle like a protective beacon of light. She lifted her hand to her forehead to block out the sun, capturing the natural painting like a photograph in her mind. Of all the years Elaine had survived in the jungle, she had never witnessed something as glorious as this.

Elaine interpreted the rainbow as a promise of all the good things to come. It gave her the hope she needed to continue on her voyage, no matter how long it might take.

Chapter 21

Frederic woke with Louisa in his arms, her head perfectly situated on his chest. His chin touched the base of his throat as he gazed down at her sleeping figure, not wanting to wake her. So Frederic laid his head back down and secured his arm around her back, soaking up the warmth of her body.

For reasons Frederic could not understand, he liked the girl. She was young and vibrant, innocence in its purest form. But he could not have her for himself, especially since the first time he ever laid eyes on Louisa had been the moment he captured her in an alleyway in New York. At the sound of her piercing scream, Frederic hated himself.

So many times in the jungle, Frederic wished that he had never taken her. How he longed to turn back time and leave the poor girl alone, provide nothing to her but love and shelter. But Frederic's father would have paid the price for that, because those were the two choices Judas had left him with. His father or the pretty blonde girl in the alley.

Had Frederic made the right choice?

Louisa shifted in her sleep and sighed aloud, pressing her hand against his torso. Lying still as a statue, Frederic stared up at the foliage overhead and rubbed her back.

He loved her.

It was a truth that he dare not utter to another soul for fear that the feeling might slip away. Everything was his fault, and he took full responsibility for her present discomfort. Frederic should have guarded Louisa with his life, because that was what he owed the poor child for capturing her in the first place. She didn't belong here, frightened in the jungle.

Louisa Rochester bore the fine complexion of a beauty queen, for she was one indeed, according to Frederic's standards at least. Her presence on the island troubled him the most, because she should have been home in Manhattan, asleep in her soft bed. Frederic had forced her on the ship that brought them all here, and he hated himself for it.

He no more deserved her love than Judas deserved a second chance.

"Henry," Louisa murmured, a gentle, hushed whimper. "Henry. No."

Frederic touched her shoulder and she startled awake, sitting upright. As Louisa came to her senses, Frederic looked her over with the care of a worried father. No matter the sacrifice involved, Frederic would do whatever it took to keep her safe. He owed it to her.

Louisa dropped her open palms into her lap and stared at the ground. Her entire body felt drained and lifeless, as if sleep had taken more than it had left. She hung her head and let her soul wither away at the realization of all that had occurred last night.

"Henry," she began, failing to make eye contact with Frederic. "Henry is..."

"Louisa, I am very sorry for your loss." He searched for her eyes but they refused to meet his. How he longed to make them shine again. Like the brilliant blue sea.

"Henry is dead," she squeaked, too tired to cry mourning tears just yet.

Frederic gritted his teeth and balled his hands into fists. Guilt overwhelmed him, seething and sucking like the poisonous venom it was. Had he never brought her here, had he never kidnapped her, had he never obeyed Judas's every command, had he...

"Do you think he is in heaven?" Louisa lifted her head and gazed into Frederic's dull gray eyes. "With Mother and Father?" She looked on with longing and waited for an answer.

Frederic moistened his lips and then pressed them together. "Yes, my dear Louisa." He scanned the features of her face without blinking, memorizing every detail. "Of course."

Louisa lowered her gaze, but Frederic's eyes remained on her. She twisted her palms together to reckon with the pain and then gasped, widening her eyes at the blood.

"Let me take care of that," Frederic offered. He took hold of Louisa's wrist and helped her to her feet, leading her away from the sheltered brush. She sought comfort in the strength of his arms and planned to never leave Frederic's side again. Louisa trusted him.

When Frederic reached a wayward brook, he crouched down and collected water to wash Louisa's wounds. While the cuts in her palms were not terribly deep, Judas had damaged her to the point of causing wounds. Frederic motioned towards a cool stone on the bank as a place for Louisa to sit. She followed his advice and held out her hands.

Frederic cupped her right palm in his and rinsed the bloody wound with fresh water. When Louisa winced at the stinging ache, Frederic kept his eyes down and said, "I'm sorry for abandoning you in the forest, girl. I shouldn't have done that."

Louisa studied the veins in his forearm and the rise and fall of his chest. Frederic clenched his jaw every time he touched her, and she was just beginning to notice.

"But I asked you to leave," she reminded him. "It wasn't—"

"It doesn't matter," he bitterly remarked,

cutting her off. "You shouldn't even be here in the first place." Frederic ripped a strip of cloth from his shirt and wrapped it around her hand. "If you are upset, take your anger out on me. I am the reason you are here, trapped in the jungle."

"But Frederic, he forced you." Louisa furrowed her brow and tensed up when the cloth brushed over the cut in her palm. "You took me, but it's not your fault."

Frederic looked into her eyes and glared. "Of course it is."

Fuming with self-hatred, Frederic washed the gash in Louisa's left palm with water from the brook, careful not to look at her. His clear disdain for her well-being left Louisa hurt and confused. Frederic had saved her life last night, and his rescue hadn't been the first.

"Frederic, I am alive because of you." She searched his face as he covered her other hand with another strip of cloth, but he dared not look her in the eye.

"You should hate me," he finally uttered, finished with mending her wounds.

"Frederic." Louisa set her hand on his shoulder even though it hurt. "I don't hate you."

"I want you to," he admitted. Unable to cope, Frederic pulled away from her and squatted down before the brook. "In fact, I wish you would."

Louisa stared at the back of his head in perplexity. "Why?"

Frederic jerked his head and gazed over his

shoulder at her. "Because you should, Louisa," he demanded. "You must." Then he splashed his hand across the water and scowled. His teeth sank into his lower lip as he shook his head in frustration.

"I was a slave, Frederic," Louisa murmured. "And you set me free."

At the sound of her words, he took a knee while smoldering.

"I owe you my life." Louisa stood behind Frederic, and when he turned to look back at her, she touched his face with her hand. "I should be thanking you, kind sir."

Withering at her touch, Frederic rose to his feet and paced back and forth, distancing himself from the girl as much as possible. He could barely resist her charms in the night. But he must garner the willpower to keep her at bay just a little while longer.

"Louisa, do you have any idea how old I am?" Frederic turned his back to her.

"No." She shook her head and frowned. "How old are you, Frederic?"

"Thirty," he said. Turning on his heel, he walked towards her and held that sweet blue gaze. "Nearly twice your age, Louisa," he insisted. "I am a man, and you are a child."

Louisa bit down on her tongue until her eyes watered. "Is that what you think of me?" she asked. "That I am just a child? Another responsibility on your shoulders?"

Frederic narrowed his eyes at her, and his nostrils flared as she moved closer.

"Well, why don't I tell you something, Frederic?" Louisa leaned in until their lips nearly touched, his hot breath joining the air with her own. "I am a woman, and you are a man." The words rushed off her lips like a sultry cadence, meant to entangle and entice.

Frederic pressed his lips together until he stopped breathing through his mouth.

"What have you to say to that, Frederic?" Louisa sassed in her own flirty way.

"Nothing, girl," Frederic barked back in resentment. "I have nothing to say."

When he stormed off, Louisa grabbed his arm before he could flee. "What are you running from?" She pulled herself closer and got in his face. "Are you afraid of me?"

"No," Frederic mouthed. "I am in love with you, and I shouldn't be."

Louisa's grasp inevitably weakened, and she let him go. As he walked away from her and took a seat farther along the brook, she dropped her hands to her sides and watched. There were tears in her eyes when he looked back at her and sighed.

She loved him too, and there was nothing she could do about it.

Chapter 22

Seven days passed before Elaine realized the likely possibility that Henry had been cast off that majestic waterfall—that is—if he had been lucky enough to land in the river. Despite the odds, she refused to give up the hunt to find Henry. So Elaine continued searching the land, even though she must have scoured the territory for the tenth time.

On her way back down the river, Elaine fell to the ground and cried. The beautiful life Henry had promised her in New York would never come to fruition. Because it had all been ripped right out from under her before the height of their life could even begin.

Giving up, Elaine lay down on the flat of her back and let the sun beat down on her skin at high noon. Her flesh had already turned brown, reverting to the tan complexion she had possessed during her youth in the jungle. Shutting her eyes, Elaine felt every tear rolling down her cheek and every stab of pain radiating through her chest.

While Elaine felt Mother Nature's light burning her skin, she contemplated what destiny must have planned for her. If Elaine jumped in the river and let it take her, she might join Henry at the bottom of his watery grave. But then an image of Lilly came to mind, and Elaine recalled that she was a mother now. What about her daughter?

With Mr. and Mrs. Rochester gone, who was taking care of Lilly? If Elaine jumped, then her daughter's chance at a life with at least one parent was gone for good. While Louisa might survive the jungle, there was no guarantee that anyone would make it off the island. Elaine had escaped once. What were the odds that she could do so again?

As Elaine lay there contemplating suicide, she opened her eyes and turned her head to the side. It was a simple task, really. All she had to do was look, and there was Henry's wedding ring. A light golden band whose mate she had once worn on her finger.

Surging with hope, Elaine crawled on her hands and knees until she reached the ring. She picked up the gold wedding band and slipped it over her middle finger. Then Elaine's fierce green eyes darted from left to right as she rose to her feet and took one step after another, eventually stumbling upon a trail of blood.

Her stomach dropped as she followed the path left by her husband. If Elaine had known how quickly they would become separated, she would have prolonged that final kiss. If given the chance, she would have done everything in her power to touch him one last time.

Elaine's heart pounded inside her chest like drums, to the extent that it knocked the wind right out of her. But she pressed onward, unable to believe that she had missed such crucial evidence during her search. When the blood ended, Elaine got down on her knees and clutched her chest. The truth was shocking: Henry had jumped.

Trembling with grief, Elaine leaned back and shrank into the fetal position. Hot tears streamed down her face with a mix of choking sobs that left her fighting for air. She looked over the edge and crouched down on her knees, biting her nails in agony and mourning.

Once the shock left her, Elaine stood up and inched her way towards the edge. Lifting her arms like the wings of a bird drifting through the air, she lowered her lashes and glimpsed the fate that awaited her down below. Wherever Henry went, she would follow.

For a moment, Elaine closed her eyes and relived every memory of her time in the jungle with Henry. She remembered their very first kiss and smiled. He was the savior she had been hoping and praying for in the jungle. But now he was gone.

Time. It was something she had resented during those lonely years on the island, because it never seemed to pass. For so long, she had been trapped between two worlds, as if there were no other existence but the lives of predators and prey in the jungle surrounding her. Now time was the one thing she wished for.

She wanted it back. She wanted it more. Time enough at last with Henry.

A cool breeze rushed over her face, as she balanced on one foot and placed the other in the river. Elaine had not made up her mind yet, but she was deciding between life and death. Clearly, it was a choice that Henry had already made without her.

As Elaine dipped her other foot in the water, a screeching cry startled her and she slipped.

"ELAINE! NO!"

With squinting eyes, Elaine made out the faintest image of Louisa in the daylight. For the slightest second, all of her nightmares were put to rest as reality set in. Louisa was alive and well, perhaps the only remaining Rochester on the island. But if Louisa was here, perhaps she had seen her brother. Perhaps she knew where he was.

Before Elaine could act on her thoughts, the current pulled hard and swift as she tumbled backwards. Louisa screamed at the sight of her sister-in-law going over with the waterfall. But there was nothing Louisa could do, because it was too late.

"NO!" Louisa ran forward, chasing after Elaine until Frederic jerked her back.

"Have you gone mad?" he yelled. "Good God, Louisa! Are you trying to get yourself killed?"

Louisa's shoulders shook as she fell down at his feet. Truthfully, she hadn't wanted to believe that Henry was gone. But now that she had witnessed Elaine taking her own life, the obvious was true. Henry was dead, and his wife wanted to join him.

"No, no, no..." Louisa sobbed, rocking back and forth like she had for Henry. "Not her. Not Elaine. Not my sister." She took a moment to think about Lilly and whimpered.

Staring across the way at the gushing waterfall, Frederic crouched down and wrapped Louisa in his arms. "Shh... Please, be quiet," he coaxed, gently massaging her back. "The last thing you want is for Judas to hear." He touched her hair and cradled her head to his chest, desperate to calm her down before death looked them both squarely in the eye.

Louisa grasped Frederic's shirt in her hand and clung to him with everything she had in her. Once he recognized that she was shaking, Frederic picked Louisa up in his arms and walked towards the cliff, hidden beneath what shadow the tall rock could provide. As he sat down with Louisa in his lap, Frederic kept calm and traced patterns over her back.

"She's dead," Louisa sobbed. "I can't believe she's dead."

"Shh... I know, sweet Louisa. I know."

Frederic breathed her in and sighed.

"But don't you understand?" Louisa sat up in his lap and swiped the back of her hand across her nose. "Elaine jumped," she noted. "That means she's going to hell."

Frederic shut his eyes and held her close until their torsos became flush. Utterly destroyed, Louisa placed her head on Frederic's shoulder and wrapped her arms around him. She squeezed so tight that he must have felt the pressure, but Frederic never complained.

When Louisa calmed down from the shock, Frederic believed all the crying had worn her out. So he set her down on the ground and brushed his thumb along her cheekbone, finding the look in her eyes to be nothing but sleepy. Frederic squatted before her and tucked a pale blonde lock behind her ear, taking care of his one and only girl.

"How about I fetch you some food?" Frederic offered. "A handful of berries might bring some color to your cheeks." He smiled, but there was no delighting her.

"All right, Frederic," she agreed. "I suppose so. If you must."

Frederic took her hands in his and searched her watery blue eyes. "When I get back, you can tell me whatever you like, Louisa. And I promise to listen."

Louisa nodded and watched him go, a single tear streaming down her cheek.

Once Frederic disappeared into the forest, Louisa pressed her back against the hard rock behind her and took a staggering breath. She crossed her arms over her chest and shivered at a sudden breeze through the trees, tangling and twisting the air around her. Her head snapped up at the sound of a popping branch in the thickets, but no one was there.

For the life of her, she could not understand why Elaine would jump. The death of Henry was a shocking blow, one that Louisa expected to mourn for years to come. But Elaine had a daughter back in New York, Henry's daughter. How could she leave her unprotected? Elaine had loved Henry, but could that eclipse a mother's love for her daughter?

Utterly empty, Louisa sat there counting the numbers in her head. Mother, Father, Henry, Elaine. Until that very moment, Louisa had failed to realize that Lilly was the only family she had left. She was an aunt now and had a responsibility to her infant niece.

Swallowing to ease the budding lump in her throat, Louisa lifted her chin and dried her eyes. She and Frederic would forge a path through the wilderness and board that ship. But not without finding Judas first. Frederic claimed to be a hunter. Louisa stared at the ground, lost in thought, imagining his capacity for hunting humans.

Something glimmered out of the corner of

Louisa's eye. Curious, she glanced across the way and spotted a long, lithe creature approaching the river. Shielding her eyes from the sun, Louisa leaned forward on her knees and felt all of the breath leave her lungs.

Beautiful creatures lingered in the jungle, but even the pretty ones needed to eat. The sleek black panther lowered its mouth to the water and lapped up a generous amount. Louisa was paralyzed by the big cat, whose dark fur coat glistened like smooth silk against the sunlight. As if it had felt the weight of her searing gaze, the panther lifted its head and those jade green eyes connected with hers, pinning her to the spot.

Louisa failed to breath, but the same paralysis had an effect on her voice. She should have called out to Frederic and yelled for his quick return. Surely he had not lingered far. Surely he would come running to her rescue. Surely he would be back soon.

Licking its jaws, the panther walked along the side of the river. With nothing but the channel of water between them, Louisa darted her eyes across the jungle, but there was no place to run. If she bolted to the right, the only place to hide was at the bottom of the waterfall. While she could have jumped up and dashed off the way Frederic had gone, Louisa simply could not move. Her limbs had turned to mush, her heart rapping loudly inside of her chest. In the jungle, nothing bore as many beautiful forms of death.

With the panther lurking across the way, Louisa hardly had a moment to think. But the beautiful creature gazed into her eyes without blinking, careful to stay on the other side of the river. Louisa felt sure the big cat would cross the water and come raging towards her. Instead, the panther shocked her and turned away, stalking off into the jungle.

When Frederic returned, Louisa was still gasping for air, her hand clutched to her chest. Frederic raced towards her and dropped to his knees, taking her face in his hands. She was shivering, as her eyes remained fixed above his shoulder.

"Louisa, what is it?" Frederic held her chin and stroked her arm.

"Did you see that?" she breathed. "Did you see—?"

But Frederic furrowed his brow and looked over Louisa as though she were mad. Turning her head to the side, Louisa stared into the jungle again and swallowed.

The panther was gone.

Chapter 23

When Elaine woke in darkness, her head was pounding and her ribs ached with the painful force of bruising. Despite the river that had broken her fall, Elaine suffered from being pulled under water and fighting her way to the surface. Once she managed to stay alive, Elaine had dragged herself out of the river and crawled across the bank, gasping and panting all the way. As she peeled her eyes open, Elaine had no recollection of exactly how long she had been on the ground at the flat of her back. But she was alive.

As a full moon hung heavy in the sky above, Elaine leaned forward to sit up straight. She felt dizzy at the sudden rush of blood to her head and shook it off. With either palm pressed to the ground, Elaine rose to her feet and stumbled towards a mountainous tree. Grabbing one of the low hanging branches, she caught her balance and sighed in relief.

But the mere act of breathing proved painful,

as Elaine pressed her fingers to her ribs. A flash of memory rushed across her mind, an image of underwater boulders scraping against her torso. Elaine winced in discomfort at the recollection and took one step forward, pressing onward into the night.

After circling the forest for hours, Elaine returned to the pool of water and sat down. She was emotionally and physically exhausted, terrified for her life and at risk of losing it at every pressing moment in the jungle. When a faint object glimmered in the moonlight, Elaine ambled in that direction and kept her eyes on the ground. In an instant, she recognized the weapon as Henry's dagger and knelt down to examine it.

Once Elaine picked the dagger up, she flipped the blade over and discovered splotches of fresh blood against the metal. Mulling over the matter, Elaine dipped the dagger in the water to wash away the excess blood, wondering what must have happened. She searched from side to side to ensure that no one was watching her in the night and then dried the weapon off on her dress. If Henry had dropped the dagger, then whose blood was this?

With newfound evidence, Elaine had no intention of sleeping tonight. So she strode along a new path, beating back lingering braches and vines. At the sight of a yellow-green snake, Elaine failed to even flinch, the soul of an islander buried deep within her.

When an owl began his nightly call, Elaine looked over her shoulder and spotted his golden eyes beneath the moonlight. He gazed down at her before taking flight, spreading his wings as he sailed through the air to another tree. Elaine watched the owl like a curious child and smiled with delight. Not everything in the jungle wanted to eat her.

But then bushes rattled nearby, causing Elaine's glistening green eyes to flood with alarm. She grasped the dagger in the palm of her hand and took a cautious step forward. When the threat rose up in the dark, Elaine crouched down low at the sight of a man.

He moved with lithe speed through the jungle, obviously on the hunt. Fear flooded Elaine's veins, as she was about to cross paths with an enemy. She could not make out his face in the dark. So when the man approached without noticing her presence, Elaine reared up and pounced on him before he had the chance to attack her.

Her unexpected visitor crashed to the ground as his back became flush with the hard forest floor. Elaine straddled his hips with one knee on either side of him and held the dagger to his throat. With the breath knocked out of him, the man gaped in astonishment.

When moonlight sliced through the trees and offered a different view, Elaine mirrored the expression on his face and gasped for air. The man lying beneath her was Henry.

Elaine gazed into the eyes of the man she loved and whispered, "Henry."

Despite the dagger at his throat, Henry stared back and relaxed. The blade fell from Elaine's hand as she leaned down and clamped her mouth onto his. Henry cradled her in his arms and met her lips with every kiss, never one to deny her affection.

"You're alive," she uttered, soft tears running down her cheeks. "I thought you were dead."

Henry braided his fingers through her dark lustrous locks, smooth as silk and black as night. When he looked up at her, Henry found the love for him that had remained in her eyes. Elaine brushed her hand against his cheek and searched every inch of his face.

"So did I." Henry placed his thumbs beneath her eyes and wiped her tears away.

"Oh, Henry." Elaine lowered her chest to his and rested her head beneath his chin. Her arms went around his torso, where she squeezed his body with constrictive force. When Henry gasped, she leaned back and tucked a black lock behind her ear.

"Careful, my love." Henry traced her lower lip with his finger and tilted her chin up. "I'm a broken man," he admitted, lowering his eyes to the fragile body she had yet to discover.

Reading between the lines, Elaine sat up on her knees and unbuttoned his shirt. She was careful in her technique, trembling with worry at the possibility of hurting him. As Elaine unfastened each button, Henry watched her every move and refused to look away.

Once his bare torso was exposed, Elaine held a hand to her mouth at the ghastly bruises and wounds covering Henry's torso. From breast to ribs, Judas must have beaten the bloody life out of Henry before Elaine found them that day. No wonder Henry had fought back with so little strength, and Judas had pushed him off the cliff so effortlessly.

Elaine gently rested her hand along his waist, as Henry looked up into her eyes. When her fingertips ran over ever nasty contusion, Henry remained still beneath her. Her gaze shifted from Henry's face to the wounds covering his body, while she wondered what to do.

"Do they hurt?" Perhaps it was an unnecessary question with an obvious answer. But Elaine had to ask it. There was a pressing need within her to know how Henry felt.

"Not anymore," he murmured, like a cool caress off his lips.

Elaine pushed either end of his shirt to the forest floor and lowered her mouth to his chest. Slowly but surely, she kissed every bruise on Henry's damaged body to heal the pain these afflictions must have caused him. When her lips left his ribs, Henry sat up and took her face in his hands, desperate to move closer and pull her near.

As Henry touched his palm to her cheek,

Elaine closed her eyes and breathed him in. The scent of Henry had been on her mind for days, because she would have given anything to have it back. When Elaine fluttered her lashes and peered up at him, Henry brushed his knuckles along the length of her throat and jawline.

Tender as ever, Henry slanted his lips over hers and slipped his hand beneath the sleeve of her dress. His fingers traveled along the dip formed where her shoulder met her neck as Henry kissed her again. Elaine unraveled at his touch and curled her arms around his back, needing Henry just as badly as he had ever needed her.

In time, Henry left a trail of kisses along her collarbone and lay her down on the grass beside him. Elaine secured her hands at the back of Henry's neck and pushed against him until his mouth met hers. As Henry slipped his hand along her thigh, Elaine tugged at his hair and sighed, crushing her lips to his with every breath.

"Henry," she called, looking up at him from the flat of her back.

He planted his hands in the ground along either side of her and looked into her eyes. "I know," he replied, acknowledging all the words left unspoken.

Henry could have died. Henry could have never seen her again. Henry could have never been given the chance to tell her he loved her one last time. So he would show her.

As he held Elaine's sensual gaze, Henry knew that the feeling was mutual. So he lowered his body to hers and covered her mouth with his, softly stroking her skin. Henry folded his fingers through hers and held her hands over her head, as they cherished every part of each other, rediscovering that old flickering flame that burned like new.

Chapter 24

Louisa gazed about in the darkness, utterly perplexed. She was at a loss for words as she rose to her feet, her balance akin to the time Judas had given her that bottle to drink. The outskirts of her vision blurred, but she pressed onward into the jungle, searching for something.

At the sound of rushing water, Louisa held on to the skirting of her dress and approached the lagoon. She knelt down before the cool blue pool and admired the crystal waterfall, glistening beneath the moonlight. Her back prickled at the strangest sensation, for she knew that someone was watching her. Some stranger lurking in the jungle.

With her heart pounding and hands shaking, Louisa slowly turned her head back over her shoulder. The black panther stood before her, its large round head close enough to touch. There was no time left to panic or flee, so Louisa remained as she was and gazed back into the glassy green eyes of the beautiful creature.

Louisa took a shallow breath as her gaze drifted from the cat's large black paws to its flickering tail. When the panther took a step closer, Louisa stiffened and felt the vein in her neck throbbing with excitement and fear. But then the animal lowered its head, breathing with patience and calm. The creature wasn't the least bit aggressive or predatory.

Following her instincts, Louisa bit her lip and placed her hand on top of the panther's head. As she began to pet the big cat, Louisa gulped at the sound of the creature purring. Adrenaline flooded her veins, but she could not turn away. She didn't want to.

Mirroring the behavior of a domestic cat, the panther lay down on the forest floor and rested its chin over those long front legs. Louisa stroked the soft fur behind the panther's ears, observing the way its smooth black coat reflected the moonlight. But then a tree limb snapped in the distance, foreshadowing the arrival of Judas in the dark.

Without hesitation, the panther rose up and glared at the intruder. Judas took two steps back and tripped over his own feet, collapsing on the ground. Turning lethal, the creature rose up and stalked forward, revealing a set of sharp white teeth determined to kill.

When the panther looked back at Louisa, it stared into her eyes and blinked. Overcome by the most absurd thought, Louisa parted her lips and whispered, "Elaine?"

Then the beautiful beast set its sights on Judas and snarled. It got a running start and pounced on him, slicing his face with its claws in the night. At the piercing cry of Judas's screams, Louisa got to her feet and scrambled out of there, hearing the terror in his voice.

"Louisa," Frederic called, his hands on her arms as he shook her from the dream.

Startling awake, Louisa sat up and caught her breath. Her blue eyes searched about the slice of jungle she could make out beneath the shelter, her palms glistening with sweat.

"You had a dream, girl." Frederic brushed the stray blonde hairs from her face and stroked his fingertips along her cheek. "What is it?"

Louisa clamped her hand around his wrist as her line of sight drifted from his mouth to his eyes. "There was a panther with black fur and green eyes. I believe it was Elaine."

"Nonsense," he declared. "It was merely a dream. Now go back to sleep."

"No." She shook her head and pushed him away. "I know what I saw."

Determined and fearless, Louisa crawled out of the shelter and approached a tree, gazing about the forest. The black panther was real, because she had seen it in the flesh at the river today. Just like tonight, the creature had not harmed her. But why?

"Louisa, come back," Frederic called. He abandoned the shelter of branches and leaves in pursuit of her, placing his hands on his hips once he reached her side. "What is it?"

Louisa turned back to him and stared into his eyes. "Judas is going to die on this island," she confessed. "I know it." She took a step closer and breathed, "I've seen it."

"Very well." Frederic shrugged his shoulders. There was no harm in her believing it.

"I saw that panther today," she recalled. "The same one from my dream."

Frederic searched her eyes and studied every inch of her face as she spoke.

"When you were gathering berries, the panther looked right at me, Frederic." Louisa pointed at her face to make the action clear. "But it did not harm me. Just like tonight."

Determined to find the black jungle cat, Louisa turned on her heel and took off. The creature was her friend, loyal enough to eliminate her enemies. If she wanted protection from Judas, the panther was the only way to ensure it.

"Louisa, stop!" Frederic chased after her and grabbed her arm. "Where are you going?"

"To find Elaine," she barked back, struggling against him. "Now let me go!"

Frederic loosened his hold, but kept his hand wrapped around her arm. "So let's see here. You believe that your sister-in-law has been reincarnated into a black panther?"

"Yes," she hissed, nodding to drive the point home. When he chuckled, she lowered her eyes to the floor and exhaled. "I know how it sounds. You think I'm mad."

"No, I don't." Frederic moistened his lower lip. "I think you had a dream."

"I did have a dream," she argued, raising her voice. "But it was real."

Frederic bit down and clenched his jaw. The action showcased the prominence of his cheekbones along with the strong nature of his jawline. He looked into her eyes and stared.

"Now let me go." Louisa tilted her head back and glowered up at him.

"I can't do that," he said, grasping her other arm gently.

"And why not?" She nearly spat at him for the way he took control. It was her body, her life, her risk, her choice. If she wanted to run off chasing an elusive jungle cat in the night, then she should have the freedom to do so.

"It's too dangerous out here in the wilderness, Louisa." His hands drifted to her shoulders so he could hold her still at a better angle. "How many times do I have to rescue you before you will believe it? I left you once, and I'm not doing it again."

Louisa held her jaw taut and scowled, utterly loathing him with contempt.

"I won't let you out of my sight," Frederic vowed, cupping her cheek in his hand.

"Why not?" Heat rushed through Louisa like a flickering flame.

Frederic leaned his forehead against hers and whispered, "Because I don't want to."

Louisa drew in a quick breath of air as her eyes settled on Frederic's full, lush lips. He took her face with delicate care and covered her mouth with a slow, yet steady kiss. Flooded with tingling emotion, Louisa tilted forward until her hands landed on Frederic's chest. His fingers tangled and twisted through her long blonde hair as he tugged at her lower lip, sealing her mouth with the sweet, renewing warmth of a first kiss.

When Frederic broke away for oxygen, Louisa clasped his hand and braided her fingers through his. Smiling at her affection, Frederic lifted her chin with his forefinger and gazed across her beautiful face. "You are so young," he softly crooned.

Blushing warmth rose to the surface of Louisa's cheeks. Even though she refused to say it, Louisa had never felt this way before. During his stint as Captain William Pierce, Judas had been cold and distant for the most part. Any affection from him had been forced and difficult to obtain. Recognizing her previous denial, Louisa accepted the fact that William had never wanted her as much as she wanted him. Could Frederic be different?

"Come lie down," Frederic beckoned, brushing her golden locks over her shoulder.

"All right." Louisa tightened her grip around his hand and squeezed. Perhaps it had been the mistake of a fool to trust Frederic so implicitly, the very man who had captured her. But her kidnapper was the same man who had set her free.

Frederic led Louisa beneath the underbrush, where they sought shelter every night in the forest. She lay down beside him and placed her head on his chest, cherishing the feel of his hand around her back. Safe in his arms, Louisa closed her eyes and draped her body across his torso. With Frederic by her side, she could finally rest.

Chapter 25

Henry tucked a lock of raven black behind Elaine's ear and placed a flower in her hair. When she smiled, he leaned down and brought his mouth to her lips. She looked so beautiful lying in the grass in her white dress, her complexion golden and clear.

"My wife," he murmured, planting a kiss on the back of her hand. In truth, Henry could hardly believe that she was his. No matter the circumstances in the jungle, as long as they were together, that was all that mattered. If only Lilly were here as well.

"My husband," Elaine answered. She brushed her hand over his beard and recalled the New York City preference of a clean shaven gentleman. "I've missed this."

Henry held her close and kissed her neck. "So have I," he whispered in her ear.

Growing weary, Henry lay down with Elaine in his arms and closed his eyes. She placed an elbow in the grass and propped up so she could watch him sleep. As his chest rose and fell with every breath, Elaine framed the long dark hair around his face.

Since she first met him, Henry had aged. The memory of an adolescent boy had been permanently wiped away, while the strong, masculine features of a man had replaced it. Henry was more handsome now as the father of her child, rather than just her friend, lover, or husband. Elaine could not explain it, but creating new life with him had expanded the sentiment. Somehow, she loved him more than one heart could hold.

When he drifted off, Elaine sat back on her knees and watched him. But then something caught the corner of her eye, and her head popped up to catch whoever had been spying on her. Discovering a lurking shadow in the darkness, Elaine stood up and slowly wandered deeper into the jungle.

Elaine looked back over her shoulder to make sure that she could still see Henry from where she stood. Then she reached two equally bounteous trees and placed her hand on the first to steady her balance. Once Elaine took another step forward, a black panther with alluring green eyes stepped out and revealed itself before her.

Breathless, Elaine cocked her head to the side and gasped. "Jade?"

The panther approached Elaine and rubbed its

head against her waist. In pure disbelief, Elaine rested her palm on the panther's back and stroked its smooth fur coat. When the panther purred in delight, Elaine petted the top of her head and behind her ears.

"Jade," Elaine called, kneeling down before the sleek cat. "I don't understand."

Acting herself, Jade crouched down on her belly and spread her paws with a yawn. When she placed her long front legs in Elaine's lap, there was nothing for the latter to do but cry. So Elaine sat there with her feline friend and rubbed her head while she purred.

Elaine whispered to Jade in the night and told her of the many struggles Henry had encountered. When Judas came to mind, Elaine revealed that he was back. Jade blinked and then gazed into Elaine's eyes, understanding the presence of evil immediately.

"I've killed him once," Elaine noted. "I can do it again."

Jade rose up and smoothed her head against the palm of Elaine's hand one last time. Then the big cat turned and walked off into the night, her long black tail swaying from side to side. Before she disappeared from sight, Jade looked back over her shoulder at Elaine and sighed. Elaine could have sworn she saw Jade smile, because this was goodbye.

Elaine opened her eyes and found Henry asleep on the grass beside her. Furrowing her brow, Elaine looked all around but the black panther with green eyes was nowhere in sight.

"It couldn't be." Elaine sat up and planted her palm on the ground.

The sound of her voice woke Henry as he stirred and fluttered his lashes. Leaning back on his elbows, Henry caught the look of worry in her eyes and asked, "What is it?"

"Jade." Elaine slapped the ground beneath them. "Jade is back! I saw her."

Groggy and confused, Henry turned his head and searched the evening jungle. "You saw her when? Just now?"

"Yes," Elaine hissed, darting her eyes across the forest floor.

With a resounding sigh, Henry took her arm and left his eyes on her face. "Elaine, I understand how difficult it must be for you, back here on the island, in the jungle. But—"

"I saw her," Elaine demanded. "I'm not crazy."

When Henry failed to believe her, Elaine stood up and stormed off. She didn't care if it was too good to be true. She didn't care if her husband thought she had gone mad.

"Elaine." Henry chased after her and grabbed ahold of her elbow. "Jade is dead. You saw it with your own eyes. Judas killed her. We left her body in the jungle."

Elaine ripped her arm from his hold and narrowed her eyes at him. "Just like I killed Judas? Just like we left his body in the jungle?" Then she turned on her heel and left.

"Elaine, wait." Henry followed her footsteps and pulled her back to him. "What are you saying? That it's possible that somehow Judas and Jade have both risen from the dead?"

"I never said it made sense, Henry," Elaine replied. "I know how it sounds."

"Well, what do you plan to do?" Henry posed, letting her go. He crossed his arms over his shoulders and searched her transfixed face. What had happened in her dreams?

"Louisa is alive." Elaine brought her glistening green eyes to his. "I saw her just before I fell. She was there at the waterfall. But I think someone else was with her."

Henry sighed with relief and relaxed his shoulders. "Thank God she is alive."

"I know." Elaine tilted her head back and looked up at the stars, taking a breath.

"Who was with her?" Henry pinned his eyebrows together, wondering. "Judas? Or that other man? The one who...? What was his name?"

"Frederic," Elaine answered. "His name is Frederic."

Henry gritted his teeth and growled, "What has he done to my sister?"

Fearing the worst, Elaine bowed her head in silence. "I don't know."

"Tomorrow," Henry decided, nodding at the idea. "Tomorrow we will find her. There is no telling what Frederic has done to her." He lowered his voice. "And he will pay."

Already in agreement, Elaine wrapped her hands around his arm and stood beside him. "What about Judas? I left him on the ground, unconscious. But you know he must still be alive." Her green eyes scanned the thickets of the jungle surrounding them. "In these woods."

"We will find him and kill him."

Elaine put her head on his shoulder and held him close, because she knew that he meant every word. "Which one?" she wondered, circling her palm over his chest.

"Both of them," he responded. "Frederic first. And then Judas."

"How?"

Henry stared up at the moon and smoldered. "We'll think of something."

Chapter 26

J udas gazed through the palm fronds at Louisa's sleeping figure. She curled into Frederic's body, and the sight made Judas sick. Flaming with red hot anger, he sucked back another bottle of rum and glared at the two of them asleep in the distance.

When he could no longer bear the sight, Judas rose from the ground and shoved off like a sloppy drunk. He ripped his fingers through his matted hair and ended up on the beach with his bare feet in the sand. La Fleur Noire lingered on the shoreline, as Judas wondered why everyone but him had retreated to the jungle.

With Henry taken care of, the only task left was to find Elaine. That island girl. With those glossy black locks that he longed to run his fingers through. And green eyes so gorgeous that they could have passed for gems.

Elaine was the one Judas wanted. And while he despised the fact that Louisa had sought comfort elsewhere, Judas could tolerate the fact that she was still alive. Frederic must have been her rescuer, another pawn in the grand chess match he was winning.

With a dead husband, surely Elaine would come running back into his arms. Though that had yet to happen. In truth, Judas wanted Elaine to be more than a puppet.

She could be his lover, wife, bearer of his heirs. Judas had no intention of returning back to civilization, so hopefully Elaine had kissed New York goodbye. Their home belonged on the island now. With Elaine's help, they would live as kings and queens in their own private paradise.

Judas supposed Frederic and Louisa could stay, make a homestead of their own. The ginger-haired lad was a fierce hunter, the best in the county from where Judas had plucked him out of obscurity. He supposed Frederic's poor father must have still been imprisoned there, his captor waiting to hear word from Judas before Frederic Holmes, Sr. could be set free.

It truly was a shame, all the energetic lives that had gone to waste. Frederic could have achieved great things, were he not compelled by the honorable notion of freeing his father. Judas sat down in the dirt until the waves washed over his feet. There was much to be discovered on the island. To be honest, hidden treasure was only the half of it.

* * *

Louisa jerked in her sleep and sprang up, gazing through the openings in the branches around them. Call her crazy, but she could have sworn someone had been watching them. Someone who looked an awful lot like Judas.

"What is it, dear Louisa?" Frederic traced patterns over her back and then tugged at a lock of her hair.

"Nothing." She lowered her bright blue eyes and shook her head from side to side. "I thought I saw someone. Or something." A sudden spurt of pain burst forth in her temple, so she touched her fingertips to the spot to ease the discomfort.

Frederic lay back down and stared up at the slivers of blue sky that the overhead shelter allowed. What if Louisa thought she had seen the jungle cat? A black panther with green eyes, according to the features she had described.

There was no denying the fact that Frederic loved Louisa. She was sweet and innocent and good, all the things that he was not. Frederic knew there was no way on God's green earth that he could have Louisa and keep her forever.

Was it so awful that she was the one he wanted? That he no longer wished to live the life of a bachelor the moment he had seen her face. Frederic wanted everything with Louisa. Marriage. A stable home. Children.

Frederic imagined a life for himself that he had never cared to dream about before. One where he could come home to a freshly cooked meal at night and find Louisa in the kitchen. Two boys playing in the floor, while Louisa placed her hand on her belly to ease the kicking of the one on the way. Perhaps a little girl. And he would spoil her in all the many ways a pauper couldn't.

But what was Frederic thinking? He lifted his hand from Louisa's back and admired her as she looked out into the jungle with fear in her eyes.

Louisa was young and inexperienced, just sixteen. She had yet to learn the cruel ways of the world. How poverty left you with nothing but emptiness. How easy it became to steal when there was no other choice but to starve.

Frederic had done things in his life. Terrible things. To protect his mother. To save his father. To feed his starving siblings. Responsibility had always been left up to Frederic. He was the eldest.

But no matter how much he thought of Louisa's best interest, he couldn't deny wanting her. He wanted to lie down beside her every night. He wanted his children to look up at him with her eyes. He had told her that he loved her. And those were words he thought he would never say to any woman.

Even if by some miracle, Louisa felt the same way, they were still stranded in the middle of the jungle. How would they escape? How would they survive?

In terms of Judas, Frederic was just a slave. One wrong move and the death of his father was imminent. Frederic had taken the deal a long time ago, but he had never anticipated that he would meet Louisa.

Frederic was ashamed to admit it, but he had watched Louisa for three days and nights before taking her in the alleyway. He had followed her. He had stalked her. But Judas had told him to.

What would Louisa ever want to do with a street rat? Frederic had seen the mansion where she lived, the carriage that took her from place to place, the elegant clothes she wore in the city. The painful truth was, in this world or the next, Frederic Holmes never had a chance with a girl like Louisa Rochester.

But he loved her anyway.

Lost in her own world, Louisa looked deep into the forest utterly transfixed, practically hypnotized. She parted her lips for the intake of breath and crawled out of the underbrush. Despite Frederic's cautious tone, she put one foot in front of the other and followed the black cat.

"Louisa?" Frederic scurried after her at the first sign that she was in a trance. She walked on with slow, careful footsteps, her eyes glued to something in the distance, something he had not seen yet.

When Louisa froze in her tracks, Frederic followed suit and looked past her shoulder. His gray eyes widened and shivering heat slithered throughout his body when he saw what she was staring at. A sleek black panther with glistening green eyes.

"Do you think I've gone mad now?" Louisa said under her breath.

"No," he whispered back. Louisa took a step forward, so he grasped her arm. "Where are you going?" Frederic demanded, holding her back.

"Wherever she tells me to."

Chapter 27

I s this where you saw her last?" Henry walked alongside the river and gazed back at the waterfall that had nearly killed him. A shiver crept through his spine. Even though the blood was on Judas's hands, Henry wouldn't make that mistake again.

"Yes." Elaine waded through the water until she was standing on the other side. "She was right here when she saw me."

"How did she look?" Henry had to know, because the moment he found Frederic, the man who had dragged Louisa off into the forest, he was going to kill him.

Elaine pursed her lips and exhaled aloud. "I can't be sure. She seemed surprised to see me. I wonder if she thought I was going to jump."

"Were you?" Henry countered.

"No. Of course not." She squatted before the river and dipped her fingers in the water, then shamefully admitted, "I thought about it though."

Henry crouched down so they would be at eye level, even with the distance between them. "Why?"

Elaine stiffened at the question, because it felt like Henry was judging her. "Why do you think?"

Henry set his light brown eyes on her and waited. His love was distressed, and she absolutely ought to be. But he had to know how his loss had made her feel. Had the separation been as painful for her as it had been for him?

"Because you were gone, and nothing else mattered."

At the affirmation of her pain, Henry crossed the river to be by her side. When he sat down beside her, his hand reached out to touch her without him even thinking about it. It was an involuntary reaction to her presence.

Henry pushed her long black locks over her shoulder so they hung down her back. Then he smoothed the pad of his thumb along her neck until her eyes slid shut. Leaning forward, Henry pressed his lips to the throbbing pulse point beneath her jawline and took pleasure in her sigh.

As his mouth forged a path down her body, Elaine grabbed the hair on his head and pulled. Henry gazed into her eyes and saw flaming hot desire there. She leapt into his arms and pinned him to the ground, hovering above him.

"We must stay focused, Henry." She kissed the corner of his mouth and then the other. "No distractions." Then she touched her lips to his and whispered, "Think of Lilly. Think of our daughter."

Henry sat up with Elaine in his lap and planted his hands at the small of her back. "You are right, my love." He rubbed the end of his nose against hers and then blessed her mouth with a soul-stirring kiss. "For Lilly."

"For Louisa," Elaine added.

Henry looked up at her from beneath his dark lashes and uttered, "For Jade."

Equally flattered and stunned by his belief in her vision, Elaine took Henry's hand when he offered it. Together, they approached the horrendous cliff that could have been the demise of Henry. A chill crept through Elaine at the memory of Judas and his eager readiness to leave Henry at the edge and push.

"Where do you believe she has gone?" Henry wondered, unwilling to scale the rocky cliff just yet.

Elaine turned around and looked off into the nearby forest. Could she be here? Hidden somewhere with Frederic's hand over her mouth to prevent her from crying out for help?

"She is your sister, Mr. Rochester. Perhaps you should be the one answering that question," Elaine murmured, saying the words soft and slow.

"Why yes, Mrs. Rochester." Henry straightened his arm against the rock and pulled her eyes to his. "But you are a woman," he pointed out. "And so is she."

Elaine smirked and rosy warmth stained her

cheeks when he stole a kiss. It had been so long, that Elaine was learning her husband all over again. One week in the jungle and three months on the ship. Another night and she wouldn't have been able to bear it.

Either separation had lasted far too long. The first was unbearable, because she thought she would never see him again. The second, because she thought he was dead.

"I believe she is above." Elaine lifted her head and pointed at the top of the cliff. "Most likely with that man, Frederic."

"What makes you say that?" Henry wondered in idle curiosity.

Elaine fluttered her eyelashes at Henry and said, "Just a feeling."

"All right, my love." Henry patted her shoulder and tilted his head back. "I suppose we have a mountain to climb."

Following his line of sight, Elaine lifted a hand to shield her vision from the sunlight. While the cliff was no mountain, it might as well have been. Elaine took a breath and sighed, wincing at the barbaric heat and every bit of pain to come.

"Sturdy enough," Henry remarked, testing out tree vines. They hung low to the ground and slightly resembled rope. If anything, those scraggly vines were the only leverage either of them had at the moment.

Since there was no need to prolong the inevitable, Elaine grabbed the first vine and lifted herself in the air. When the pads of her feet hit the sweltering rock, Elaine gritted her teeth at the discomfort and began walking her way up the side of the cliff.

In no time, Henry scaled the rock alongside her, as they each griped and gasped. It was an unpleasant journey to the top. But once Elaine pulled herself over, Henry appeared stuck at the cliff's edge.

"The rock," he rasped. "It's cutting into my ribs."

Alarmed and alert, Elaine lay down on her stomach and reached out for Henry. When her nails dug into the flesh beneath his arms, Elaine feared that she was only hurting him. But then she pulled hard enough for him to make it over the edge and land on top of her.

All of the air traveled to the back of Elaine's throat with his sudden weight on her body. Henry placed his knees on the ground and planted his hands along either side of her face. "Sorry, my love. I did not mean to hurt you."

Elaine lay breathless beneath him and gazed into his eyes. When his pupils dilated, thinning out those golden irises with black, her heart swelled with joy. Henry leaned down and covered her mouth with a long, tingling kiss. Due to the circumstances, they had to make the best of their love while there was still time left to do so.

"You bewitch me, darling," Henry whispered against her mouth. "You always have."

Elaine lifted her lips into the faintest smile, hardly a grin. Then she stroked his cheek with tender care. "I've always wanted you," she confessed. "From the moment you washed ashore and I found you bloody and wounded. I wanted you to be mine."

Tears filled Elaine's eyes for the life they could never get back again. The one in New York City, and the one before that, in the jungle.

"I am yours," Henry gently whispered. "And you are mine. Always."

Collecting herself, Elaine let Henry's words wash over her and soaked up the sweet sentiment with joy. Henry got to his feet and then leaned down to help her up. "I'm sorry," she muttered, seemingly out of the blue.

"For what?" Henry held one of her hands in his and weaved his fingers through her hair with the other.

"The time I told you to build a boat and get off my island." She broke down in earnest sobs. They flowed freely after holding them back for so long. "I never wanted you to leave," she confessed. "You have no idea how desperately I wanted you to stay."

"Shh... Quiet, my darling." Henry kissed her forehead and clasped both of her hands. "Save your tears for another time. They won't help you now."

Elaine knew he was right, but couldn't shake the feeling that something terrible was about to happen. It was just like the night she had given birth to Lilly, only the premonition felt much stronger this time. Maybe because the danger was so incredibly close.

"We will find those men and kill them," Henry declared. "And then we will take Louisa and go home. All right?"

Elaine nodded in reply. "All right," she said, as she dried her eyes.

"Now, first." Henry rested his hand on her shoulder and looked all around. "Do you have any weapons?"

"Just an empty pistol," she answered.

"Do you have it? Let me see," Henry urged, growing anxious and impatient.

Elaine removed the gun from the skirt of her gown and handed it to Henry. He uncovered a dagger of his own, the one she had found last night before discovering him. Apart from fighting physically, the empty pistol and dagger were all they had.

"Well, I suppose it could be worse," Henry admitted, trying to stay positive. "Give me the pistol. You take the knife."

"But Henry—"

"Do as I say, Elaine." He lowered his voice and leaned in closer. "Trust me."

Despite her indifference, Elaine clasped the dagger in her hand and watched him take the gun. Perhaps he could fool Frederic or Judas into thinking it was loaded. At least that was what

Elaine assumed he must have been thinking.

With the turn of his heel, Henry strode into the jungle and they were off. Elaine stayed by his side as every move was both careful and deliberate. They crouched down low at the first possible noise, only to discover that it had been made by an animal every single time.

When they reached a makeshift shelter of branches and greenery, Henry slowed to a stop at the unusual occurrence in nature. Someone must have built it with his bare hands. Henry spotted a piece of cloth on the ground and knew immediately who: Frederic.

Smoldering with fury, Henry picked up the cloth and smelled it. Then he handed it to Elaine and she did the same. They both knew what had happened here.

"That came from Louisa's dress," Henry assumed. "Did it not?"

Elaine failed to answer the question, because he already knew the answer.

"Do you think he brought her here?" Henry asked.

"Yes."

"Do you think he tortured her?" Henry loathed the mental image, but had to know what she thought. Elaine knew men of the wilderness better than him.

"Yes."

"Do you think he touched her?"

Elaine searched the surrounding jungle for any

signs of a voyeur. "Henry, I really don't think—"

"Do you think he touched her or not?" he snarled, his blood hot and boiling. "Just answer the question, Elaine."

She flicked her tongue out to moisten her lips and then said, "Yes."

It may not have been the answer Henry wanted to here. But it was the honest one, so that made it the right one.

Caught up in a tumultuous rage, Henry lost all control and obliterated the shelter of branches. He stomped his way through every square inch of foliage and beat the limbs until they twisted and snapped. Dust flew in the air and muddled Henry's eyes, but he did not care.

With the shelter destroyed, Henry panted aloud until his breathing steadied. Dust settled to the bottom, but he kicked the structure one last time. Elaine placed her hand on his shoulder and gave him the piece of cloth from Louisa's dress.

"Are you ready?" she asked.

Henry snatched the cloth from her hand and wiped his mouth with his shirtsleeve. "Yes."

Chapter 28

The black panther gazed back over her shoulder and waited for Louisa and Frederic to follow. With idle curiosity, Louisa chewed on the edge of her lip and memorized those glistening green eyes. They reminded her so much of Elaine.

Before she could wander off without him, Frederic took Louisa's hand and braided his fingers through hers. She flitted her blue eyes up to meet his gray ones and nearly melted over the way he was looking at her. Frederic rubbed his thumb against the heel of her palm in reassurance, letting her know that he supported the decision she had made.

Frederic touched her cheek and declared, "I'll go with you." When Louisa smiled, it warmed whatever shred of a heart he had left. He wanted to be wherever she was.

The panther growled as Louisa snapped her head back to look. Impatiently waiting, the big black cat turned her back to them and walked off.

Frederic and Louisa shared a look before following the alluring creature through the jungle.

Frederic remained on the lookout during their trek through the forest, darting his eyes this way and that. The jungle cat led them to the easternmost part of the island without looking back. With her long, lean frame and those sharp fangs and claws, in an instant, Frederic and Louisa could become dead meat.

But Louisa relied on her intuition and felt safe with Frederic by her side. If he were not here, she would have followed the beast into the jungle anyway. Louisa couldn't be sure if the realization was good or bad.

Frederic clamped his hand around Louisa's arm and pulled her back when a swarm of birds flew overhead. Louisa looked up and caught her breath as the fluttering creatures disappeared across a tapestry of blue sky. When Frederic released her arm, she relaxed but longed for the squeezing strength of his touch again.

The black panther weaved her way through the forest without missing a beat. Certain to catch up, Louisa hurdled forward in a rush. But Frederic wrapped his arm around her waist to steady her and keep her a safe distance away from the creature.

Minutes passed as Frederic and Louisa carried on, following the tracks of the big black cat. While Frederic had never believed in reincarnation, he was starting to wonder at the friendly nature of this creature. What if Elaine had passed on to another life? What if she was leading them right now, while she grew used to life in the body of a panther?

Feeling the tension of Frederic's swirling thoughts, Louisa kept quiet as the panther led them on and on. After a while, Louisa worried that following the jungle cat had been a mistake, that she never should have trusted her instincts, that they might have been wrong. But then something in the demeanor of the cat changed, and Louisa braced herself.

With ears pointed and paws forward, the panther arrived at a pool of water. Unlike the lagoon, river and waterfall, the liquid was not clear. After twitching her tail from side to side, the big cat lay down and glanced up at Louisa.

Confusion set in as Louisa leaned in closer and knelt down at the edge. She wrinkled her nose at the acrid smell and looked on in intrigue. Despite the sour stench, the visual appeal of the water was awfully sweet.

Frederic stood behind Louisa and quirked his brow at the spring. The outermost ring of water was aqua blue and also the widest. A circle of vibrant green sat at the center, a deep color the exact shade of the greenery in the jungle. Frederic cocked his head to the side at the odd occurrence in nature.

Unable to resist her curiosity any longer, Louisa reached out and dipped her fingers into the water.

"Louisa!" Frederic crouched down to grab her arm, but she pulled back just in time.

"It's warm," she revealed, rubbing the pad of her thumb across her fingertips.

"We must go," Frederic warned her. "I fear the water is not safe."

Louisa shut her eyes with a sigh. When she opened them again, the panther lay by the spring, looking at her with docile green eyes. Open minded, Louisa stared back at the cat, and when she turned her head to the water, Louisa took note.

"I think she wants me to go in." Louisa rose and tugged at Frederic's shirtsleeve.

"What on earth for?" Frederic clasped her elbows in his hands as a means of keeping her safe.

"Something is in there." Louisa nodded her head towards the colorful spring. "She wants me to find it."

Frederic widened his gray eyes at her in disapproval. "Absolutely not, Louisa. It's too dangerous."

Louisa held her head high and withdrew from his grasp. "You are not my father, Frederic."

"Louisa," Frederic scolded. "I can't bear the thought of anything happening to you." He took her face in his hands and brushed his thumb against her cheekbone. Inside, Louisa tingled at the touch, but she could do without the distraction at the moment.

"If you don't let me go now, I will come back later in the night when you are asleep," Louisa declared. "I want to know what is beneath the water. You will not stop me." She touched her hands to the backs of his and lovingly gazed into his eyes, appreciating his obvious concern for her safety. "I am not asking for your permission, Frederic."

When he opened his mouth to speak, Louisa leaned up on the tips of her toes and kissed him. She had never been the one to initiate a kiss before. But loving Frederic was easy, because he had been the only one to let her go free when she was chained.

"Trust me, my love," Louisa spoke against his mouth. It was the first time she had used the term of affection. Frederic gazed down at her and sighed. He had told her he loved her, and Louisa was essentially confessing much of the same.

"But you could—"

"Would you rather I come back in the night? Alone?" Louisa squeezed his arm. "You just stay here and watch me," she suggested. "If anything happens, you'll be right here."

"All right dear, sweet Louisa." Frederic grinned when blush warmed her cheeks. "I'm not going anywhere."

"Good." Louisa beamed up at him and then found the panther's green eyes on her. Swallowing, Louisa moistened her lips and took a breath.

Frederic followed Louisa's line of sight and

looked over his shoulder at the panther.

"Turn around," Louisa commanded.

"What?" Frederic replied, caught off guard.

"Turn around, I said." When he failed to move, Louisa spun his body in the opposite direction with a breathy laugh.

Rolling his eyes, Frederic exhaled aloud and put one hand on his hip while the other hung freely by his side. When he looked down and noticed the panther laying just a few feet away, he stood up straight.

Unaltered by his presence, the panther crossed her paws and rested her head on top of them. With Frederic's back to her, Louisa took the opportunity to lighten her current display of clothes. After unfastening the appropriate buttons, Louisa slipped out of her dress and tossed it on the grass. Her underclothing would do, as she still wore a thin white slip from the night Frederic had captured her in New York.

Bracing herself, Louisa took the first step forward and ran her fingers through her hair. Then she got close enough to dip her toes into the water. It felt warm and reeked of brimstone, but she had no intention of stopping now.

Louisa moved deep enough into the water for it to reach her waist. Feeling around for the bottom, she swished her feet back and forth like a pair of scissors. Then she moved from the outer blue ring to the center of green. It was such a strange reflection of light, for when she puddled water in her hand it was neither blue nor green.

"You may turn around now, Frederic," Louisa chimed, paddling to keep her head above water. She inferred that the centermost part of the spring must have also been the deepest.

Frederic turned around and watched young Louisa floating in the water, her blonde hair slicked back and wet. She was beautiful, like an elusive siren or mermaid sent to take his soul. With the way she smiled at him, Frederic accepted the fact that it was already hers.

"How does it feel?" he asked.

"It's cooler in the center," Louisa observed. "Why do you suppose that is?"

"I do not know, my love," Frederic shrugged. "Now, why don't you climb out of there? You've had your fun."

Something sparkled beneath the water and Louisa flinched. "Wait," she protested. "I saw something."

An electric eel or venomous snake was the first worry to come to Frederic's mind. "Louisa, that is enough." Frederic stayed at the edge and extended his hand. "Get out of there."

Defiant by nature, Louisa looked up at him one last time and then dipped her head beneath the water.

"Louisa!"

She heard the sound of Frederic's frantic voice as she descended down below. Swimming with all her might, she kicked her legs and propelled herself into the depths of the spring. As she swam lower and lower, it had never occurred to her exactly how deep the water might be.

The farther Louisa swam, the darker everything around her became. But then she spotted a flicker of red in the distance and pushed deeper. Forgetting that she was underwater, Louisa gasped at the sight and it became a struggle to breathe.

Above the surface, Frederic paced back and forth, unsure of what to do. He was just about to jump in after her when the panther rose up on her haunches and peered into the water, dangerously close to the edge.

Bubbles rose up from the emerald core, as Frederic and the panther could do nothing but watch and wait. When Louisa broke the surface gasping for air, Frederic leapt into the water after her. She coughed and gagged, fighting her way to the outermost ring of blue.

Once she reached it, Frederic grabbed ahold of Louisa's body and dragged her out of the water. She was cold and shivering, leaning her face into Frederic's warmth. Terrified for her life, Frederic wrapped his arms around Louisa and pulled her into his lap.

"What happened down there, Louisa?" Frederic touched her head and pushed the damp locks out of her face. "What did you see?"

Relishing the warmth of his palm to her face, Louisa opened her mouth and looked into his eyes. Then she leaned her head down and opened her hand. Diamonds, rubies, and a necklace fashioned of pure gold and sapphire slipped out from her palm.

Astonishment flitted over Frederic's features as he turned back to Louisa to hear her say, "Treasure."

Chapter 29

It was late afternoon by the time Henry led Elaine to the westernmost part of the island. They had yet to come across Louisa, Frederic, or even Judas. But Henry would scour the whole jungle if it was necessary to find his sister.

"Water, Henry." Elaine pointed to the mouth of a delightful brook as they reached the edge.

Pleased with the discovery, Henry approached the brook and was thankful to be in the shade. Elaine knelt down and cupped the water in her palm. After a satisfying drink, she splashed the cool liquid over her face. Relishing the calming feel, Elaine smoothed the wetness of her hands along her hair, as Henry joined her for a sip.

Lounging on the ground, Elaine embraced the moment of relaxation with her husband. It was a much needed break from the danger that surely awaited them. As Elaine sat there quietly, she stared at her husband in honest admiration.

"I love you, Henry."

At the sudden affirmation, Henry ceased from patting water along the nape of his neck and looked back at her. Not liking the sound of her voice, Henry took a knee before her and held her hand. "Elaine, I—"

"I just wanted to say it," she interrupted. "One last time. In case something happens to—"

"Listen to me, Elaine. Nothing is going to happen. To either of us." Henry braced her shoulders and then turned her chin up with his forefinger and thumb. "Nothing. All right?"

Elaine nodded with a pretty pout.

"We are getting off this island," Henry declared. "I promise you that."

When her lower lip trembled, Henry sealed her mouth with a kiss. She whimpered at the pleasure as a salty tear streamed down from her eye. Henry threaded his fingers through her silky hair and laid her down on a bed of grass.

Elaine wrapped Henry in her arms and curled her legs around his back. As he left a string of kisses down her neck, Elaine tilted her head back and sighed. That elusive feeling was back. The one that told her danger was imminent.

* * *

Gently rocking her body, Frederic stared down at the gems and gold. "Where did you get that?"

"In there," Louisa murmured, pointing at the spring.

"You must put it back." Frederic went to stand

up, but Louisa squeezed her arms tighter around his rib cage so he wouldn't let go.

"Why?" Louisa set her bright blue eyes on Frederic and waited for an answer.

Frederic bit his lip and curled his finger around a lock of her hair. "If someone left it there, you don't believe they have the intention of coming back to it?"

Hearing reason in his words, Louisa curled her arms around his neck and replied, "I'll put it back. But I'm cold. Just hold me a little while longer."

Frederic pressed his lips to her forehead and then tucked her head beneath his chin. She shivered as he held her close, rubbing her arms to keep them warm. Louisa had such smooth, soft skin, and Frederic treasured it helplessly.

"How many women have you loved?" Louisa lifted her angel eyes to meet his cloudy gray irises.

Ashamed, Frederic hung his head, and his Adam's apple bobbed. "You don't belong with me, Louisa. I'm no good for you."

Tears filled Louisa's eyes as she tugged at his auburn locks. "But I love you."

Frederic shook his head and pressed a finger to her lips. "You shouldn't say such things, girl. You are only a child."

With her heart breaking, Louisa turned away from him in embarrassment. But Frederic coiled his arms around her and pulled her back into his chest. He hoped that his words had not hurt her, but knew that they must have.

"Don't cry, my darling," he coaxed.

"You told me that you loved me." Louisa lifted her hand to her mouth and felt Frederic's beard brush against the side of her neck.

"I do love you," he whispered. "But we could never be together."

Louisa wept, wanting her mother, wanting her father. She longed for Henry and Elaine. But they were all dead.

"Don't you see?" Frederic grabbed Louisa around the waist and turned her towards him. Then he searched her eyes and set her down across his knees. "If we make it off this island and return to New York, I will go back to my life and you will go back to yours."

"I don't have a life," Louisa sobbed. "My family is dead. Don't you understand?" She stroked his beard and admired him through her tears. "You are all I have left."

Frederic curled her little body into his and wrapped his arms around her, hugging her close. As she rested her head on his shoulder, Frederic rubbed her back and said, "One day, you are going to meet a good man. You will love him, Louisa. And he will spoil you tremendously."

"I don't want a good man," Louisa cried. "All I want is you."

"Please, Louisa," Frederic begged. "Try to understand. It's what is best for you."

Lifting her head from his shoulder, Louisa stared into Frederic's eyes and asked, "Then why does it hurt so much?"

Frederic searched her innocent face, feeling an equal amount of pain. "Because it just does." He waited a beat and then added, "I'm only here to protect you and keep you safe."

Louisa pulled away from him and struggled to her feet. She dried her tears and gathered the pieces of treasure off the ground, swiftly tossing each one back into the spring. As she pondered the probability that the jungle cat had known what lay at the bottom of the spring, Louisa turned around and gasped.

The panther was gone.

* * *

Blissfully sated, Elaine twisted her fingers through Henry's hair and kissed him as he refastened the buttons on his shirt. Henry touched her cheek and molded his mouth to hers. Then he reluctantly slipped the dress over her head and pulled the fabric down to cover her body. Elaine had a subtle glow about her, and Henry loved the fact that he had been the one to put it there.

Feeling euphoric, Elaine set her knees alongside either of Henry's hips. She placed her head on his chest and curled her arms around his torso, holding him close. Henry reciprocated and squeezed her tight, while they stayed that way for a very long time.

Elaine set her chin on Henry's shoulder and looked off into the distance. Black smoke rose up and swirled over the treetops in the sky. "Henry?" she called. "What is that?"

Henry secured his arm around her back to keep her in his lap and followed her line of sight. He saw sweeping feathers of smoke and furrowed his brow. "I don't know," he replied. "Why don't we go take a look and find out?"

Her mood inevitably altered, Elaine pulled Henry close and shuddered.

Chapter 30

H enry took Elaine's hand and led her to the smoke. What a fool Judas or Frederic must have been to light a fire in broad daylight. His only motive in forging down this path was the chance that Louisa might be waiting on the other side of it.

"Where is it coming from?" Henry wondered, lifting his hand to shield his eyes from the sun.

"There." Elaine pointed to a mountainous tree up ahead. "If we climb up there, we'll be able to see."

Henry smiled at her keen eye and placed a kiss on her cheek. He let go of her hand and watched her go on ahead of him, admiring the smooth, fluid way her hips moved when she walked. When she turned back to Henry and called out his name, he hurried to catch up to her.

Without hesitation, Elaine grabbed ahold of the lowest branch and swung herself to the higher one beside it. Pulling her feet up, she climbed the tree while Henry crept up behind her. Once she reached the top, Elaine stopped and stared. Her reason for astonishment was clear, because she had discovered the source of the smoke.

Henry lifted himself up and stood behind Elaine, following her finger in the direction it was pointed. He looked straight ahead and realized what all the fuss was about. Before them, seamlessly hidden on this very island, was an active volcano.

"Wouldn't Judas hate to find himself in one of those?" Henry caught Elaine's gaze, not caring if she thought him dark as of late.

"You have a plan," she assumed.

"Yes, my darling." He kissed her head and whispered, "I do."

At the sound of a cat-like snarl, Elaine darted her eyes down. A black panther with green eyes stood at the bottom, flicking her tail back and forth. Elaine tugged the collar of Henry's shirt, so he could see with his own eyes that Jade was back from the dead.

When Henry looked at the panther, the creature stared at the couple only a minute more before disappearing into the jungle.

"Do you think I've gone mad now?" Elaine declared.

Henry climbed down from the tree but failed to answer. Rolling her eyes, Elaine swung from branch to branch. If only her husband would just admit the truth. That she was right.

Confused by what he had just seen, Henry

trekked on through the forest. He lifted his head high to examine the volcano from where he stood. What was the best way to lure his enemies inside?

"Jade is back," Elaine announced. "Jade is alive."

Henry kept walking and ignored her, too distracted by his need for revenge. Judas would pay for his sins. And so would that Frederic. He would pay for all the wicked things he had done to Louisa.

"Why won't you admit it? Now that you have seen her with your own eyes?" Elaine placed her hands on her hips and watched him staring up at the sky from afar, the distance growing between them.

Without taking his eyes off the volcano, Henry said, "Perhaps she had a daughter."

Just like that, Judas emerged from the thickets, held a knife to Elaine's throat, and aimed a pistol directly at Henry.

Elaine let out a cry for help, but Henry froze in his tracks. No matter what move he made, her life was at risk. What could he do?

"Shh..." Judas whispered in her ear. "Quiet down now, love."

Henry should have thought twice about it, but he could not help moving towards her.

"Another step, young Henry, and I'll cut her throat." Judas tightened his hold on Elaine and cocked the gun at Henry. "You have a set of choices before you, my love."

Elaine cringed at the feel of Judas's breath against her neck, while hot wet tears streamed down her face. Before he even spoke, Elaine knew what his intentions were.

"Your body or his heart?"

Henry raced towards Judas with a vengeance. "NO!"

But Judas fired the pistol and shot Henry in the leg. Elaine cried out in agony as Henry crumpled to the ground. The knife against her throat tightened, and she could hardly swallow. Judas knew what choice she would make.

"Don't go with him, Elaine!" Henry shouted, gritting his teeth in pain. "Dammit, don't go!"

Judas fired again, but Henry rolled over and missed the shot.

"STOP!" Elaine yelped. "Please, let Henry be."

"You have made your choice, island girl?" Judas rested his chin on her shoulder and kissed her neck.

"Yes," Elaine croaked, gazing at Henry. She looked into his light golden eyes and whispered, "I'm sorry."

Despite the agony of his gunshot wound, Henry lurched forward and crawled towards Elaine. But Judas rose up and kicked the heel of his boot against Henry's forehead with so much force that he blacked out.

"NO!" Elaine cried, seeing Henry unconscious on the forest floor.

But Judas had no mercy, quickly dragging her off to the nearest tree. When he knocked her to the ground, she rolled over and kicked him in the gut with as much force as she could muster. In no time at all, Judas had flipped her onto her stomach and smashed her head into the dirt.

While he ripped the fabric of her dress, Elaine looked up and saw Henry lying on the ground. She shut her eyes and squeezed them tight, because she did not want to think of Judas every time she saw Henry's face. So Elaine covered her eyes once she had them closed and braced herself for the worst.

Triumphant to have rendered Henry and Elaine helpless, Judas set the knife down on the ground. Then he placed the pistol alongside it with a chuckle. Husband and wife had been foolish enough to believe that the gun was still loaded.

Judas touched the back of Elaine's leg and she shook with fear. Just as he lifted the hem of her dress, a strange silence fell over the island, like an eerie calm before the storm. In tune with his surroundings, Judas lifted his head just in time to watch the volcano explode, and red hot lava gushed across the island.

Tell Me Your Favorite Part!

If you enjoyed Island Smile, I invite you to head over to Amazon and let me know your favorite part. Reviews are so important to an author's career, because they help new readers like you discover the book. Even if you didn't enjoy Island Smile, I'd still love it if you could take three minutes to let me know what you think of the book.

Leaving a review is super easy:

1) Go to Island Smile Book Page on Amazon

2) Scroll Down and click "Write a Customer Review"

3) Sign in to Amazon if prompted

4) Select a star rating

5) Write a few short words (or long words, I won't judge)

6) Click the 'submit' button

I thank you in advance!

Acknowledgements

First of all, I would like to thank my awesome, amazing parents for believing in my dreams from the very start. You guys read my stories back in high school when I never imagined they would materialize into much. Thank you for cheering me on at every turn. You'll always be remembered as my original fans. Back when Tom and Addie were no more than a secret kept between the three of us.

Special thanks to my extended family and friends for the much needed breaks from my crazy writing schedule. Sometimes all I need is some popcorn and a movie. I can't think of anyone else I would rather break bread with after a long day. Y'all keep me sane ;)

Thank you to Kylie, George, and Jeananna at Give Me Books. You lessen the stress of Release Week and spread the word to those who don't even know my name. To all the bloggers/reviewers who sign up for every event, you guys rock! I would never be able to get through Cover Reveals & Release Blitzes without every single one of you. So thank you!

Susan Meachen at Authors & Readers Café: You have absolutely rocked my world with your love for *An Arrangement*. I cannot thank you enough for spreading the word about Benny and Claire. I never imagined so many people would have that story in their hands, and I am overwhelmed with the positive feedback it has received. Thank You <3

Rose & Margie at Can't Stop Reading Blog: Thank you for letting me do my first ever Author Takeover with you lovely ladies! I appreciate your support in helping me spread the word with upcoming releases. Rock On! :)

I would also like to thank SJ's Book Blog, Kylie's Fiction Addiction, Reading Between the Wines Book Club, The Howling Turtle, Sassy Book Lovers, More than Scribbles, Celtic Lady's Reviews, Lisa Loves Literature, Nerd Girl, Love Books, Sapphyria's Book Reviews, Word Spelunking, Socrates' Book Review, Paulette's Papers, Mrs. Mommy Booknerd, Rolo Polo Book Blog, Keep Calm and Write On, I Read Indie, A is for Alpha B is for Book, Penny for My Thoughts, Yah Gotta Read This, Amazeballs Book Addicts,

Who Picked This? and any of the other awesome bloggers out there that I might have missed. Y'all are awesome :)

To the lovely authors I have met out there in indie world including Jessica Hernandez, Lauren L. Garcia, Aubrey Parr, Amanda Leigh, India R. Adams, Tee Smith, Micalea Smeltzer, Molly E. Lee and Addison Moore. Every one of you deserves a huge shout-out, and I look forward to watching y'all craft new stories in the years to come.

Last but not least, I would like to thank you, the reader. You are the lifeblood of my journey as an author, and without you I would never have the opportunity to turn my daydreams and fantasies into full-fledged novels. However you came across my name, thank you for reading and experiencing the world of *Island Smile*. I hope Henry and Elaine brought some light into your day and helped you escape to the jungle, even if it was only for a little while. Much love, hugs and kisses to you all... :)

About the Author

Lindsay Marie Miller was born and raised in Tallahassee, Florida, where she graduated from high school as Valedictorian. At sixteen, she started writing her first novel, *Emerald Green*, after being inspired by Stephenie Meyer's International Bestselling *Twilight Saga*. During her time in college, Lindsay wrote 5 more novels and over 100 songs. After graduating Summa Cum Laude from Florida State University, she put her B.A. in English Literature to good use and published her debut novel, *Emerald Green*. An author of over 10 Romance Titles, Lindsay currently resides in her hometown of Tallahassee where she is always working on her next novel.

To learn more, please visit:

www.lindsaymariemillerauthor.com

Sign up for Lindsay's newsletter:

lindsaymariemillerauthor.com/claim-your-free-book/

Join Lindsay on Facebook at:

facebook.com/LindsayMarieMillerAuthor

Follow Lindsay on Twitter at:

twitter.com/Lindsay_MMiller

Here's a sneak peek of

COASTAL SPIRIT,

the highly anticipated conclusion.

Chapter 1

W hat was that?" Louisa turned back and looked off into the distance, gazing through the trees.

Frederic walked in a straight line and lifted his head to the sky. Billows of smoke danced and swirled across a tapestry that belonged to the clouds. A strange breeze drifted through the trees, lightly jostling every green leaf.

When Frederic looked back at Louisa, she draped her arms over her stomach in a comforting hug. He knew that he had chosen the wrong time to say those things to her. That they could never be together. That she was all wrong for him. That he loved her anyway.

But Frederic only wanted to protect her from a life of worry. Days spent trapped beneath a ceiling of poverty. If they ever made it back to New York, Frederic refused to entertain the thought of a life with Ms. Louisa Rochester. He had nothing to offer her, and she deserved the whole world. He could not marry Louisa, because she would just end up hating him in the end if he did.

With her blue eyes burning bright, Louisa gazed up at Frederic and waited. She waited for him to say he was sorry, that he never meant any of those things. She waited for him to draw near and hold her close. But he did not, and Louisa failed to understand why she was filled with just as much surprise as disappointment.

"Why don't we look for that cat of yours and find out?" Frederic grinned at Louisa, but she did not return the expression.

Instead, she brushed past him with her head down, resenting the fact that her body trembled when it came so close to his. She cupped her elbows in her palms and heard his footsteps at her back. A single tear streamed down her cheek, her last one, as Louisa sought out whatever had been the source of that explosive sound.

After five minutes of silence, Frederic could not bear the absence of her smile. "Louisa," he called after her. But she neither stopped nor turned to face him.

Frederic stared at the back of her pretty blonde head, knowing that he would never be able to get her out of his. She was just a girl, a child, just sixteen. But he couldn't help viewing her as the beautiful grown woman that she was destined to become.

"Louisa!" Frederic rose his voice, and she hurried her steps in retaliation. She refused to let him see the way his words had affected her. She would rather die than give him the pleasure of watching her in pain.

Soon, her quick march transcended to stomping, and she wasn't even embarrassed by it. Perhaps he should have thought twice before plunging a dagger straight through her fragile heart. Metaphorically speaking, of course.

"Louisa!" Frederic repeated for the third time. "Will you just wait?"

She ignored him and marched faster, wanting to be away from the man who had claimed her broken heart. Somehow, this was worse than discovering that Captain William Pierce was actually a pirate named Judas. His affection for her had been a fraud, but Frederic's was real.

Frederic grabbed her arm and pulled her back, holding her wrists when she squirmed. "What would you prefer? That I lie to you?"

"Yes," Louisa snapped. She attempted to scurry away from him, but he would not let her go.

"So you'd love a liar then?" he challenged her, smoothing his thumb along the inside of her wrist.

"I would rather believe that you hate me with every fiber of your being than know that you love me and we cannot be together."

Frederic released her and blinked the sunlight from his eyes. "Fine." Then he took a step closer at the very moment she took a step back. "I hate you," he said. "I hate your long blonde hair and your blue eyes." His hands came around her face as he tilted her head back. "I hate the way you look at me. I hate the way you smile."

As her lower lip trembled, Frederic brushed his finger against the plump, soft nature of it. She stood there helpless and vulnerable before him. Her heart was beating so fast that it melted her insides to the consistency of sweet honey and molasses.

"I hate the way you say my name," Frederic went on. Her eyes were locked on his, and he knew that was where he wanted them to be. Always.

Louisa shivered, because the blood beneath her skin was pulsing with delight. "Go on," she softly requested. "Please."

Frederic threaded his fingers through her hair and brought his face closer to hers. "I hate the way you say I love you."

Louisa was glued to the spot by the earnest look in his sparkling gray eyes. They almost looked metallic today. Like silver.

"What else?" she whispered.

"I hate the way it feels to hold you in my arms at night."

"How does it feel?" she wondered, her voice turning soft and sweet.

"Like heaven," he crooned, gently caressing her skin.

Louisa whimpered at the very moment Frederic molded his mouth to hers. Her fingers traveled across the fabric of his shirt, and his chest tightened at her touch. Frederic was delicate and tender as he angled her face to meet every kiss.

Longing for the body of the girl he could never have, Frederic let his hands drift to her waist. When he pulled back an inch to let her breathe, Louisa cooed. Her eyes remained closed but she smiled, clinging to the collar of his shirt.

Frederic rubbed his hand over Louisa's hair and grinned when a fresh shade of blush stained her cheeks. Sinking her teeth into her lower lip, Louisa opened her eyes and stared into Frederic's. She could not help herself when her gaze immediately landed on his mouth. Her heart thrummed against her chest, and Louisa knew that she wanted him to kiss her like that again.

But something caught Louisa's eye, as she reluctantly pulled her focus from Frederic for a moment. In the distance, molten hot lava was searing across the land, melting everything in its path like candle wax. "Frederic," she gasped, tugging at his sleeve.

Frederic followed Louisa's line of sight, and his eyes shot wide open with alarm. A gushing lake of lava came rushing towards them. "Run!"

Paralyzed by the sight, Louisa faltered in her steps, fumbling about from the very start. Frederic grabbed Louisa by the arm and dragged her after him. But she looked back, mesmerized by the thick viscous nature of running lava.

"Louisa, let's go!" Frederic barked. "Come on!" He sprinted through the trees, twisting her arm when she failed to run fast enough.

"Move!" he shouted when the lava nearly touched their heels.

At the first sign of the ocean, Frederic darted to the left and yanked Louisa after him. He cut through the jungle and slipped out of the lava's path just in time. When they reached the sand on the beach, Frederic checked over his shoulder to make sure they had dodged the line of fire.

Louisa let go of his hand and stumbled to the ground on her hands and knees at the shoreline. She coughed and grasped her stomach, worried that she might gag. A sleek sheen of ice cold sweat coated her skin at the thought of drowning in scorching hot lava.

Frederic waded out into the ocean and sat down beside her, letting the salty waves rush over them. They exchanged a look that communicated every word they had yet to say. Louisa sailed into his arms and held on tight, still struggling to catch her breath.

Pulling her in closer, Frederic stroked his fingers through Louisa's hair and cradled her head to his chest. When she calmed down, Frederic kept her tangled in his embrace. Then he looked back and spotted the purging volcano off in the distance.

Still shuddering in fear, Louisa crawled into his lap and dug her nails in at the back of his neck. Frederic relaxed as she placed her head on his shoulder and breathed in and out. Like a coping mechanism for the potential death they had just skirted around. In truth, the volcano had been one of many close calls that never seemed to be very far away.

How many lives did they have left? How many more times could they cheat death? How many days remained on the island for them to survive?

Chapter 2

Fleeing like the coward he was, Judas hopped to his feet and took off into the jungle. Rather than racing towards the beach, he rushed inland. Perhaps he believed that the deeper he plunged into the forest, the greater his chance of survival.

Relieved, yet confused by the sudden departure of Judas, Elaine sat up on her knees. Her hands were shaking and unyielding fear trembled through her body. When she turned to look back, Elaine's mouth hung gaping open and her eyes widened in shock. Lava skied down the volcano with precision and speed, quickly making its way towards them.

Sure to be quick, Elaine glanced down and spotted the knife and pistol on the ground. Judas had been enough of a scared fool to run off and leave without them. She scooped the weapons up in her hands and hurried over to Henry with them.

"Henry," she called, shaking his shoulders. But

he would not wake up. "Henry!"

Elaine peered over her shoulder, but the lava had yet to filter through the trees. Regardless, it was inevitably on its way and heading towards them. Fast.

"Wake up, Henry!" Elaine cried, trying her best to stay strong and not fall apart. When he made no movement, Elaine darted her eyes over his peaceful face.

Henry was unconscious and bleeding with a gunshot wound in the leg. If Elaine couldn't move him, the lava would swallow him whole and he would be buried alive.

"HENRY, PLEASE!" She begged, jerking his arms and shoulders. "Wake up, my love. Please, wake up."

When Henry lay still, Elaine flicked her eyes up at the rushing lava in the distance. Then she turned back to Henry and slapped him across the face. But even that would not rouse him from his state of sleep.

"Dammit, Henry," Elaine muttered, her teeth clacking together with fear. She reached over and grabbed the dagger, then sat back on her knees and looked at him. "I am sorry, my love." Elaine molded her mouth to his and then fought through the tears in her eyes. "I'm sorry."

With a shaky hand, Elaine opened Henry's palm and sliced the blade along his skin. At the sudden pain, Henry shot up and yelled. He glanced down at his bloody hand and turned to

Elaine in shock.

"Get up!" Elaine commanded when his right foot made contact with the ground. The bloody gunshot wound in his calf was pulsing and red. "Come on, Henry. Move!"

Gritting his teeth, Henry clung to Elaine's arm and hopped forward on his left foot. He limped on the right, not daring to bring the full weight of his body down on it.

"Henry!" Elaine squealed, as a sea of fiery orange lava came rushing towards them.

Elaine dug her fingernails into the back of Henry's shirt and tore her eyes away from the volcano, pushing onward through the jungle. Despite his agony, Henry felt the bordering heat and took off on his bare feet. With every step, Henry clenched his teeth so tight that he thought they might crack. But he would rather watch the bone in his leg pierce through his skin than drown in a hot lake of fire and lava.

Ducking and weaving through the forest, Elaine clamped her hand onto Henry's arm and refused to let go. When they created enough distance, Elaine turned back and looked over her shoulder at the all-consuming, molten hot liquid fire. Henry sat down in the grass, yet to be touched and charred by the volcano. It was somewhat fascinating to watch a sea of blood and fire, for that was how it looked. It sent a chill up Elaine's spine, and even though the lava was flaming hot, she felt terrifyingly cold.

"We must go, Henry." Elaine knelt down and clasped Henry's elbow, thankful that they had missed the lava lake. If Henry had remained unconscious, Elaine had no clue how she would have been able to save him. Henry had a gunshot wound that needed to be treated. Lacking confidence, Elaine worried that she might not possess the skills to mend his wound. Unlike the time Jade had flayed Henry's torso with claw marks, a bullet was currently in his body, saturated in his blood.

So many things could go wrong. What if the injury became inflamed? What if the injury became infected? As her mind raced with fear, Elaine wrapped Henry's arm around her shoulder and let him lean into her body for support. She curled her arm around his waist and led him through the forest, while Henry hopped on one foot, sweating with discomfort and fear.

A cool breeze drifted through the trees as Elaine looked out for the approaching sea. Henry gasped and grunted, struggling to carry himself along. How she longed to have the strength of a grown man, someone who could lift Henry up and carry him to shore. But Henry was simply too heavy for her to do anything more than drag him. Since he insisted on hobbling his way there, Elaine filed the possibility away as a last resort.

"Elaine." Henry winced, a fine line of sweat streaking down his face. "I must stop to rest."

Concerned for her husband, Elaine slowed to a

stop and eased Henry into a seated position on a flat stone. When his posterior connected with the rock, Henry dug his heels into the ground and leaned back with a hiss. Then he flicked the stray pieces of dark hair from his face and lowered his head to examine the gunshot wound in his leg.

Not wanting to rush Henry, Elaine crouched down before him and rubbed his arm to provide some sense of comfort. When he looked up at her, fear flitted across Henry's light golden eyes. Perhaps he had already begun to consider what his future life may hold.

"Henry," Elaine called, taking his face in her hands. "Let me take you to shore. I can mend it. Just like the time you were attacked by Jade when you first arrived on the island."

Licking his lower lip, Henry looked off into the distance and then settled his gaze on Elaine. "Yes, but your jungle cat did not have claws made of bullets."

Elaine hung her head and squeezed his arm. She had already thought as much, but was too afraid to say anything to him. Should he drown in the helplessness of doom?

"I know, Henry." Elaine got down on her knees and peered up into his eyes. "But I can fix it," she assured him. It was stretching the truth, but how could she frighten him? How could she entertain the thought of the damaging effects of that single bullet?

"Thank you, my love. But what about

infection?" Henry smoldered.

"Henry, I can prevent it from being infected. It is still early on."

Henry shook his head and growled. "Oh, really? And how, Elaine? You are not a doctor. You have no medical experience," he snapped, raising his voice.

"I know, Henry," she spoke in a still, small voice. "But I can—"

"What? What can you do?" he shouted, alarming Elaine. "Forget infection, darling. What if it becomes gangrenous? Have you ever thought of that?"

"No, I hadn't thought of it." She bowed her head in supplication, praying for a sense of healing calm to drift through his body. In all honesty, she had thought of it. But she was just so happy to have escaped the volcano and still have him alive. For now, at least.

"We are trapped here on this godforsaken island, and I could very well spend my final days here as a man with one leg!" Henry yelled, his face flushed with red ripe anger.

Her skin prickled at the sound of his words. In all their time as man and wife, Henry had never frightened Elaine to such a degree. She had known of his temper from the moment he arrived on the island, but never expected to hear such rage as this.

Henry refused to see light in the matter, letting nothing but darkness filter his thoughts. As warm tears streamed down from Elaine's eyes, she swiftly wiped them away with her fingertips. There was a hole in her chest where her heart used to be.

"Elaine." Henry reached out to touch her shoulder, but she moved away.

Letting her raven black locks fall in her face, Elaine rose to her feet and walked several steps away with her back to him. She shut her eyes and took a deep breath, picturing the life she had envisioned them to have. It was surely a fantasy now, no more than a dream. Henry and Elaine in New York with little Lilly in a stroller on a warm spring walk in Central Park. The mental image shattered, and Elaine broke down into sobs.

Sinking to the ground, Elaine touched the base of the nearest tree and wept. She got down on her knees and leaned into the trunk, finding more warmth in the wood than her husband could provide. A thick lump nestled at the bottom of her throat, tangling and twisting her stomach into knots. All Elaine really wanted to do was scream.

Henry braided his fingers together and stared at the ground. When he looked over at Elaine crying, turmoil ripped through his heart, because he had hurt the one he held most dear. He pressed his fingertips against his temple and let out a sorrowful sigh.

"Elaine," he called, but there was no reply. "Elaine, I'm sorry."

Elaine tilted her head to the side, though only enough for her to hear him. Then she tucked a lock of hair behind her ear and flitted her eyes across the forest floor.

"Darling," Henry whispered, seeing the fault in his outrage. "Please."

Elaine bit her lower lip and trembled, butting her forehead against the palm of her hand. After making love to Henry and then nearly being raped by Judas, and fleeing a sea of lava from the volcano only to realize that her husband may never walk again, Elaine's sheer sanity was moments away from shattering. She was a mere human, who could only bear so much.

Henry stood up and hopped over to the tree by Elaine. Despite the pain in his leg, he leaned into the trunk and took a seat behind her, plagued with guilt over what he had said.

"Elaine," he called, resting his hand on her back.

She flinched at his touch, which made him resent his actions all the more.

"Forgive me, darling," he gently crooned, brushing her hair over her shoulders. "I didn't mean what I said. Any of it. Can you just forget that I said it? I was upset."

Feeling mellow, Elaine sniffled at her sobs and took a deep breath.

Henry wrapped his arm around Elaine's stomach and placed his head on her shoulder. "I never want to hurt you," he reminded her. "Please believe me, my love."

Still shaking with the fear of losing him, Elaine

turned back and fell into his arms. Henry rubbed her back and held her close, making a mental note to never let his booming rage explode like that before her again. After all, how often did he have to run from lava?

Elaine stroked her fingers along the nape of Henry's neck and leaned back to look at him. "I thought surely he would kill you, and if you knew what he was about to do to me..."

Henry touched her hair and held her head up with his hands. "What did he do to you?" With a pounding heart in his chest, Henry pressed his thumb against her chin and then stroked the length of her jawline. "Elaine. Did he touch you?"

Elaine covered her mouth with her hand and cried, "Yes."

His golden eyes widened in a vengeful rage. But before he could take off on a mission to kill, Elaine grabbed the collar of his shirt until he was forced to stay.

"Not in the way you must think, Henry," she confessed. "But he wanted to. He was about to. If not for the volcano, it could have been so much worse."

Henry wiped all of her tears away and reeled Elaine into his lap.

"No, Henry. Your leg," she protested, concerned for his injury.

"Shh..." Henry brushed his finger across her lips. "I will be fine."

She looked into his eyes as he put her down on

his thigh, well away from the gunshot wound in his lower calf. Elaine gasped for air and embraced Henry, squeezing him with all of her might. Soaking up her love, Henry threaded his fingers through her hair and smelled her sweet, exotic scent. Then she brushed her cheek against his beard and sat up to look at him.

"Forget what I said before," Henry murmured. "I know you can mend my wounds."

With a tender smile, Elaine leaned in and covered his mouth with hers. Henry braided his hands at the small of her back and tugged at her lower lip, holding her body closer. When Elaine twisted her fingers through the ends of his hair and whimpered, Henry took a breath and rested his forehead against hers.

For the longest moment, they reveled in the warmth of holding each other close. Elaine could have been raped and killed. Henry could have been roasted alive. Either could have reached the end of life without the luxury of saying goodbye to the other.

When Elaine breathed him in and sighed, Henry tucked her head beneath his chin and lovingly caressed her arm. He ignored the throbbing, searing ache in his leg and channeled all of his pain towards the task of holding her close. As she snuggled into his warm body, Henry kissed her head and swept his fingers through her hair.

He was her savior. And she was his.

Chapter 3

Frederic circled his palm over Louisa's back as salty waves washed over them. She lowered her head as he traced lines across her face, his fingertips caressing every inch of skin with delicate care. Shock evaded them. Stone cold shock. And fear.

"We're never going to make it off this island," Louisa muttered. Her eyes stayed down as she contemplated the probable future laid out before her. Even if she never returned to New York City, she could still have a husband, a family, a life. Couldn't she?

"Sweet Louisa." Frederic turned her chin in his direction and willed her to look his way. As soon as he saw those innocent blue eyes, Frederic parted his lips to speak. "I wish you wouldn't say such things. You have a young, beautiful life ahead of you." Then he threaded his fingers through her hair and leaned closer. "For that is what you are."

Melancholy, Louisa turned her head to the

side and looked away from him. Tears threatened to break free and skitter down her cheeks, betraying her feelings on the inside. But Louisa fought against them and replied, "So I am worthy of a beautiful life, just not one with you." She darted her eyes up to meet his, holding her jaw taut with aggravation.

Frederic looked down at the waves around them and sighed. "You could never have the life you deserve, if you chose one with me." He took her hands and squeezed them. "Why can't you see, Louisa?" When he searched her eyes, she refused to meet his. "Don't you understand?"

"Understand what?" Louisa snapped, jerking her hands from his grasp. "That if matters were different... If I were older, If I were beautiful, If I were someone else, then what?" She narrowed her eyes at him, swallowing to ease the sudden dryness in her throat. "Then you would want me? Then I would be acceptable according to your rules?"

Frederic took her face in his hands, holding it merely inches from his own. Her eyes drifted from his full lips to his steely gray eyes, as she opened her mouth to speak.

"I don't deserve you," he whispered, struggling to get the words out.

Louisa gazed into his eyes without holding back. "I don't care."

Frederic touched her cheek and cocked his head to the side. When his fingertips descended to her neck, she lowered her lashes and sighed. But despite the pulsing desire racing across the surface of his body, Frederic felt obliged to be a gentleman.

"What do you want from me, girl?" he wondered. "You know I can never have you."

Opening her eyes, Louisa angled her cheek into the curve of his palm. "And what if we never leave this island? What if we are stranded here forever? No longer bound by the conventions of modern society. Like Adam and Eve. What do you make of us then?"

When the little angel put it like that, what was Frederic waiting for? He glanced at the deep blue sea and figured the chances of them returning home to New York alive. What if neither of them ever made it back? What if they were stuck in paradise forever? Together?

Would it be so wrong to indulge in his desire? What was so awful with the way he felt about Louisa Rochester? She was young. She was beautiful. She was innocent.

Louisa was perfectly pure in every sense of the word. From her flawless ivory complexion to those dazzling blue eyes that brightened every time he crossed her path. She was like a precious gemstone, untainted by the rough hands of another. Frederic hoped and dreamed and glimpsed his future in her eyes. But was that what she truly wanted?

Stranded on the island, Frederic could fulfill his dream and claim the one he truly loved: her.

New York City might remain a distant memory for all he knew. But the jungle posed no standards of high society. In the wild, there was no rich or poor, no young or old, no damaged or pure.

Nature, as colorful as it may seem, was black and white to say the least.

He was a man. She was a woman. There was no other point in the matter.

If Frederic and Louisa were trapped in paradise, why not find some pleasure in the pain? Why not enjoy the ever-blossoming nature of forbidden love?

Louisa touched the end of her nose to his cheek and then whispered in his ear. "I want you to touch me. I want you to love me. I want you to hold me close and never let go."

Solidified by her words, Frederic shut his eyes and treasured the feel of her lips above his neck. When he wrapped his arms around her and squeezed, Louisa trailed her fingertips along the ends of his hair and tugged. For so long, he had resisted the girl of his dreams, the angel in the night, the beautiful blonde beauty. But maybe he had been a fool.

After all, what was Frederic fighting? Desire? Lust? Attraction? The way she made him feel, because a civilization which he may never see the likes of again had led him to believe so?

Perhaps it was time to break the chain he had secured around his heart. Distance had never been intended for someone like Louisa, for she had breached the very walls and climbed straight over with the intent to mark him as her own. Body and Soul.

She had transfixed him from the very start. The young girl with the innocent blue eyes. Call it fate, destiny, or chance. But her charms were no accident.

They were in love.

"Frederic," Louisa whined, planting a soft kiss on his cheekbone.

Giving in, Frederic lifted her body up in his arms and Louisa wrapped her legs around him. Waves rolled onto the shore, crashing against them as Frederic worshipped her with a soul-stirring kiss. Louisa whimpered at the taste of his mouth and jerked at the collar of his shirt, bringing him as close to her as their bodies would allow.

Gentle and understanding, Frederic traced his hands over Louisa's back and returned his lips to hers. Despite the inevitability of what was bound to happen between them, Frederic wanted to take things slow. She would control the temperature and pacing of the undeniable passion between them. And Frederic would never take advantage of the situation or sweet Louisa. Because his wish had come true: all he ever wanted was her.

"Frederic," Louisa rasped against his mouth. "I love you."

He stilled at the sound of her words and frantic nature of her breathing. In a perfect world, Louisa would be his to keep forever and his father would be free. But when he took in the paradise surrounding them, maybe it wasn't as imperfect as it had seemed.

"And I love you," Frederic echoed.

Determined to go through matters right, Frederic put his hands on Louisa's face, and she clung to him to keep from falling out of his arms. He was so tall and strong and broad-shouldered, his body molded to muscular perfection. Desperate to receive his love, Louisa crushed her lips to his and leaned her head back when he began gifting kisses along the side of her face and down her neck. Nearly two decades alive, and all the glorious wonder of the world that she had missed. Surely, Frederic would enlighten her body and soul.

"Louisa?" a strangled, breathy voice called from afar.

Furrowing her brow at the familiar sound, Louisa lifted her head and looked up. Elaine stood in the sand with tears in her eyes, letting them stream down her face without caution. Alarm rippled through Louisa at the sight of her sister-in-law, the very woman she believed to be dead. If Elaine were still alive, then did that mean Henry...

Before she could finish her thought, Henry appeared in true living color and came hobbling towards her. Overwhelmed with joy, Louisa relaxed into Frederic's arms and beamed in delight.

Elaine was alive.

Henry was alive.

And they had found each other at last.

It was a miracle. Because now she could introduce them to her one true love, the dashing Frederic Holmes.

"How dare you!" Henry lunged forward and tackled Frederic into the ocean.

"Henry, no!" Louisa protested, but it was already too late. Her brother pounced on Frederic like wolves after a yearling. She held a hand to her gaping mouth and shook with grief as Henry pummeled Frederic and then held him down beneath the water.

"Elaine," Louisa cried, tugging on the dress of her sister-in-law. "Please. Make Henry stop. Don't let him hurt Frederic." She paused with a choking sob. "I love him."

Confused by the whole affair, Elaine looked from Louisa to Henry. Could it be that Frederic had not tortured and violated poor Louisa? Could he have beaten the odds and actually been kind? Could he have protected her instead? Maybe even loved her?

"Henry!" Elaine shouted, running into the ocean. "Henry, STOP!"

But Henry wrapped his hands around Frederic's neck and pushed his body beneath the water. The filthy scoundrel had put his hands all over Louisa. And he was going to pay.

"STOP!" Elaine waded into waist-deep water

and struggled to pull Henry back. "Stop it, Henry! You're going to kill him!" she warned, wrestling with what was true and right.

"Precisely." Henry lifted Frederic's head from the water and then dunked it below the surface again. Only this time, he had no intention of releasing his hold.

"Frederic!" Louisa shrieked. True terror flashed before her eyes as she watched her brother attempting to strangle the life out of the man she loved. As if sheer drowning weren't enough.

Unwilling to relinquish Frederic, Louisa rushed into the water and punched Henry in the face until he let go. As Frederic's body sank to the wet sand beneath the surface, Henry stumbled back and cried out in pain. Blood coated his teeth, and he could hardly believe that his own sister had broken his nose.

Elaine grabbed Henry by the arm and dragged him to shore, guiding his limping figure to the shelter of a shade tree where she could tend to his wounds properly.

Paralyzed with fear, Louisa grabbed the sleeve of Frederic's shirt and jerked him out of the water. When he fell limp in her arms, she dragged him to shore and lay his body down in the sand. Frantic and trembling, Louisa pressed her ear to his heart and then sat up to look at him. In a series of quick movements, she held his nose and performed mouth-to-mouth in a feeble attempt to revive him. As Frederic lay helpless in the wet sand beneath her, Louisa trembled and wept.

"Please, my darling. If you love me, come back to me," Louisa murmured.

When it seemed that her time had run out, Frederic finally lurched forward and coughed up water from the sea. Louisa dug her knees into the sand and beat him on the back, careful to hold him upright in a seated position.

When he could breathe again, Frederic briefly glanced over Louisa and then collapsed to the ground. He lay on the flat of his back and looked up into her eyes through the thin slits of his own. Sobbing with relief, Louisa placed her head on his chest and curled her body into his. Frederic responded to her touch by smoothing his hand across her shoulders, as she lay down beside him and listened to the sound of his beating heart.

Chapter 4

H ave you gone mad?" Elaine snapped. After removing the bullet from Henry's leg and wrapping the wound in cloth, Elaine failed to overlook his erratic behavior.

"You know as well as I do that we have had every intention of killing that man."

"Yes, but did you ever see him harm her?" Elaine searched Henry's smoldering brown eyes when he looked away. His gaze inevitably landed on Frederic and Louisa curled up in the sand together. It was a strange picture to see the sister he loved so irrevocably tied to a man he had grown to hate. Regardless of the confusion, he had only intended to protect her.

Henry scowled and ground his teeth together in frustration.

"Did it ever occur to you that he might actually love her?" Elaine suggested.

"For goodness sake, Elaine." Henry gestured his hand across the way. "Frederic could be her father. He must be fifteen years her senior at least. What do you call that?"

"Henry," Elaine scolded. "She has been completely alone on this island, because we have been incapable of finding her. That man has saved her life on more than one occasion. And yes, if you must know, she loves him. She told me so herself."

Henry brushed the matter off with a sly shrug. "Louisa is sixteen," he explained. "Just the other day, she was professing her love for Judas. Look how much of a gentleman he turned out to be. Not that she would know any better."

"But what if Frederic is different?" Elaine turned soft and sweet, lowering her voice enough to sound sultry. When Henry met her glistening green eyes, he relaxed.

"Look, Elaine. I have no intention of apologizing to that man," he confessed. "Say what you want. But he is the one who brought her here to the island and took her away from home. How can I have any empathy for her captor?"

Elaine sank into the sand and replied, "Well, I think you should speak to them both."

"Do you now?" he answered back. "And why is that?"

"Because we all want the same thing."

"And what is that exactly?" Henry held his jaw taut and groveled.

"All four of us want Judas dead."

Surprised at the connection, Henry absorbed

her words and let his arms dangle over his knees. Perhaps she was right, but how could Frederic be trusted if that were the case? Did that not make him any more than a traitor?

"Just think reasonably about this, Henry. We've been apart on the island, and Judas has gained the upper hand every single time. Imagine if we formed an alliance. Perhaps Judas can take on two at a time. But how will he face up to four against one?"

Henry sighed in disapproval and shook his head from side to side. When he turned his head to gaze out along the shoreline, he found Louisa helping Frederic to his feet. The man was tall, strong, broad-shouldered, a striking contrast to the small figure of Louisa. But as his young sister planted her hands on Frederic's shoulders to keep his balance, Henry felt something inside him shift. Perhaps he had been hasty and uncivilized. Perhaps he had imagined a violent sexual assault that never occurred. Perhaps he had been wrong.

"Elaine!" Louisa called, waving her arms about. "Would you come here please?"

Sensing the concern in her voice, Elaine tucked a black lock behind her ear and flitted her eyes across the way to take in the sight of Louisa. Hopeful, she lifted her hand to shield the sunlight from her face and then glanced back at Henry with a look of admonishment.

"Yes!" Elaine shouted back. "Will you be all right alone for a moment, Henry?"

"Yes." Henry slumped against the trunk of the tree and gestured his hand. "Go to her, Elaine. It appears I have some matters to sort through on my own."

"All right." Elaine leaned down and left a kiss on Henry's cheek. "I shall return."

As Elaine sprinted across the sand, Henry reclined against the tree and clumped his fingers through the sand. He cocked his head to the side and strained to listen once Elaine reached Louisa and Frederic. Somehow, Louisa beamed anew like a glowing ray of sunlight.

"Oh, Elaine." Louisa pulled her sister-in-law into her arms and gave her a tight squeeze. "We thought you were both dead." She closed her eyes and breathed a sigh of relief.

"What on earth gave you that idea?" Elaine took a step back to hold Louisa at arm's length. Even though Frederic remained by her side, Elaine hardly felt in the way.

"Judas," Louisa replied, swaying her posture as the wind cut through her hair.

Gazing out at the horizon, Elaine mulled over the matter and bit her lip.

"You cannot imagine the terrible things he has done to me," Louisa said.

Elaine begged to differ. "I assure you that I can," she returned.

"You have no idea how long we have been searching for you, Elaine." Louisa placed her balance on one foot and then the other, bouncing back and forth. "I thought I might never see either of you again. Thank God for Frederic."

Elaine lifted her chin and glanced over at the man. He was no more than a stranger to her.

Upon first sight, Elaine had loathed the captor. For he had been the one to assist Judas and even drag poor Louisa into the jungle to treat her in whatever way he wished.

But Louisa hardly seemed frightened of Frederic now. Elaine recognized the rushing blood against the young girl's cheeks as a sign of mutual friendship and attraction. Perhaps Frederic had never harmed her. Perhaps he had saved her. Perhaps he had rescued her.

With the way Louisa kept referring to the pair as we, Elaine understood that an irreprehensible bond had formed between them. Perhaps Frederic deserved not punishment but praise. After all, he could be the sole reason why dear Louisa was still alive.

"I would like to thank you, sir, for saving the life of my sister." Elaine held her hand out for Frederic to shake. "You have done a great service to us all. I can never thank you enough."

Still off kilter, Frederic hardly cracked a smile. But he took Elaine's hand when she offered it, not wanting to be rude. "It was no problem at all, I can assure you."

"Well, I would like to apologize on behalf of my husband." Elaine looked back over her shoulder at Henry. "After the way you dragged

Louisa off, I am sure you can imagine his thoughts. To be honest, I thought the same."

Frederic cleared his throat and swallowed. "I won't let anyone harm Louisa." Draping a protective arm around her shoulders, he pulled Louisa close and she took his hand.

Such a tender touch of affection mesmerized Elaine. Her lively green eyes dropped down to watch the way Frederic tangled his fingers through Louisa's. Somehow, amid the strife, violence and danger, the couple had undoubtedly found love. How could Elaine condemn the act? It was the same method that had led her to a happy life with Henry.

"I am pleased to hear that." Elaine regarded Frederic and Louisa with a subtle smirk.

"Have you seen Judas?" Louisa grabbed Elaine's arm. "He keeps coming after me. One night he chased us through the forest with a pistol. Then he tied me to a tree, covered my clothes in blood and left me for dead. I was nearly eaten alive by a crocodile."

Elaine widened her eyes and parted her lips. "Judas shot Henry."

Louisa took a breath and held a hand to her chest. "Is he very badly hurt?"

"I have removed the bullet and cleaned the wound," Elaine answered. "If not for the volcano, Judas would have done much worse. He has already shoved Henry off a cliff. We are lucky that Henry survived." Warm air passed through her lips. "He is lucky to be alive."

"Until Judas is dead, we are all at risk," was Frederic's earnest reply.

"Yes." Elaine nodded in agreement. "Please. Come meet my husband, Henry."

Chapter 5

P erhaps we should stay inland," Frederic suggested. "Judas will find us here."

Henry scowled and set his golden glower on the speaker. "He will find you anywhere."

Stiffening at the response, Frederic fluttered his dark lashes and regarded Henry affably. Despite a long-winded and highly plausible explanation from his own sister's mouth, Henry had yet to regard Frederic as anything more than a wayward captor. Henry could not picture the very man who had appeared to be Judas's right hand man to suddenly mold into Louisa's knight in shining armor. Apart from truth, reality, and reason, Henry disliked Frederic, because he could not trust him.

"Yes, but we are easier to spot in broad daylight than hidden in the forest. Are we not?"

"Well, you would know now, Mr. Holmes. Wouldn't you?" Henry countered.

Frederic clenched his jaw and smoldered down

at the man in the dirt. While Henry was the younger of the two, he would sooner die than take orders from a scoundrel turned hero. Henry had seen Frederic take Louisa and drag her off into the jungle. It was an image that would never sit well with Henry, because it was one that he could never forget.

"You think my experience as a hunter provides no advantage to us?" Frederic asked.

"I am still trying to reconcile with the absurd possibility that you would provide advantage to any of us," Henry fired back. "You are a liar and a thief. You stole my sister."

"Henry," Louisa butted in. "If you could only open your mind and see that you are not describing Frederic at all. He has saved my life numerous times on this island."

Henry rolled his eyes in a seething rage, his blood boiling hot.

"I would be dead if it weren't for him," Louisa went on. "Can't you see?"

"Can you see, Louisa?" Henry tossed the question back at her. "You are trusting a man who helped Judas capture you and bring all of us here to this godforsaken place."

Perplexed with doubt, Louisa furrowed her brow and began to wonder.

"We have been taken away from New York and brought here to die," Henry proclaimed. "And that man." Henry lifted a finger and pointed it at Frederic. "The one you claim to love. He is responsible for it all. His kindness has not been brought about by sympathy, but guilt." Henry watched Frederic with a smoldering gleam in his eyes.

"Henry, you must think about this reasonably," Elaine remarked.

"I have thought of it reasonably, my darling." Henry kept Frederic pinned to the sand before him with a threatening glower. "Reasonable is the only thing I am being right now."

Elaine threaded her fingers through her hair in frustration and exhaled.

"But, Henry," Louisa piped up, her voice a breathy, shaky sigh. "I love him."

Narrowing his eyes in disapproval, Henry looked from Louisa to Frederic and then back again. "You love him?"

Henry had heard as much from Elaine, but failed to believe her at the time. Could it be true? That his innocent little sister had fallen for the guilty man in the wild? Perhaps it was easy to believe. After all, Louisa had also expressed similar regard for Judas. Her feelings may have been untainted and true, but they were not good. Loving a man like Frederic or Judas was quite simply dangerous.

"Yes," Louisa cooed, weaving her fingers through Frederic's once she took his hand. "We are in love, Henry. It happened in the forest. Frederic loves me, too."

At the sight of their fingers interlocking, Henry

leapt up and tackled Frederic to the ground. "She is young and naïve," he growled. "And you touched her!"

"No! Henry! Please. Stop!" Louisa reached out, but Elaine held her back.

"I never harmed her," Frederic explained. "But I do love her."

Henry had his hands wrapped around Frederic's throat, but something in the man's silvery gray eyes made him stop. As much as Henry wanted to pummel Frederic into the ground, how could he take away Louisa's only source of joy? If he were lying, surely Louisa would say so now that she had been reunited with family. So why had she failed to utter a single word of his hostile treatment towards her? Was it because a violent attack had never occurred? Because Frederic had never violated or touched or harmed her?

Had Frederic been telling the truth? That he truly loved her?

As honesty flooded through him, Henry sat back on his knees and released Frederic. He looked over the man's body and observed the fresh marks he had left on his neck. Perhaps malice and vengeance for Judas had clung together and swirled through him.

Henry was desperate for revenge, desperate and bloodthirsty. Perhaps the evil of the jungle had crept into the veins beneath his skin. He was not the same man.

"I am sorry I struck you," Henry muttered, though he failed to make eye contact with Frederic. "Forgive me." He rose and hobbled towards the shade tree. "Forgive me."

Frederic lay on the flat of his back in the sand, still panting for air. Slowly but surely, Henry limped his way farther down the island, to the place where the shack had once been.

"I must go to him," Elaine said. "Look over Frederic, will you?"

Louisa nodded and watched Elaine trudge after her brother. The sun was setting in the distance, streams of red and pink blending beneath the cool blue water. As a shudder drifted through her, Louisa knelt down in the sand to care for Frederic.

But then she paused to look back over her shoulder at her brother across the way. Despite her reluctance to admit it, the truth was startlingly clear.

Something was terribly wrong with Henry.

Chapter 6

The moon hung pearly white over a flat tapestry of black as waves crashed against the shoreline. Henry rested beneath the shelter of two beach trees just past the border dividing the jungle from the sand. After setting his nose, Elaine had sat with him for hours in the hope of persuading Henry to forgive Frederic and accept him as a member of the island.

But Henry remained quiet and apathetic, crossing his arms over his chest in resentment. As Elaine left his side to join Louisa by the fire, Henry glowered at Frederic in the distance. He had been fooled, tricked, and betrayed by men in the past who were just like him. Frederic associated with pillagers and pirates. There was no change of heart.

Needing a break from Henry, Elaine reached Louisa and settled down beside her in the sand. Frederic had speared fish earlier in the evening and steamed them over the fire for everyone to eat. As Louisa handed Elaine a piece of meat, she took it with delight and scarfed down the heavenly substance. Elaine could not remember the last time she and Henry had consumed a proper meal, hardly scraping by on coconut milk and berries.

"This is wonderful, Frederic," Elaine crooned, sinking her teeth through the flesh.

He smiled at her from across the flames, his knees tucked into his chest as his arms dangled over his legs. Aware of the awkward tension in the atmosphere, Frederic glanced several hundred feet away and caught Henry's stern, aggressive gaze. There was anger in his light, golden eyes for the transgressions of Frederic's past.

But Frederic had no way of traveling back in time and leaving Louisa untouched. If he had not taken her, they never would have met, much less fallen in love on the island. Yet Frederic knew Henry would not accept the fault of fate or destiny. The fault of Louisa's kidnapping rested on Frederic's shoulders, and so must the punishment as well.

"Perhaps you should speak to my brother, Frederic." Louisa placed her hand on his shoulder and squeezed the tensing muscle there. "Surely, he has calmed down by now."

With a reluctant sigh, Frederic nodded his head and went to stand. He had figured as much while Louisa and Elaine sat there eating the fish he had caught for them. Dinner had been an attempt to restore trust with Elaine and establish it with

Henry. Yet Henry kept his distance and refused to eat, revealing how little trust he had in Frederic.

"Keep the fire low," Frederic recommended. "Wouldn't want to alert Judas."

"Yes, my love." Louisa lifted her head up as Frederic leaned down to gift a kiss on her cheek. "Don't let him be too harsh on you. He doesn't understand. You have done nothing wrong."

Frederic wasn't so sure that he agreed with that, but he nodded anyway and let go of her hand. Surprised by Louisa's term of affection, Elaine darted her eyes between the pair with a smirk on her face. When Frederic walked away and headed towards Henry, he heard the sound of Elaine whispering in Louisa's ear and wondered what she had to say about him.

His arms hung limply by his sides on the journey to see Henry beneath the beach trees. Frederic may have been nearly five years older, yet Henry startled him with the sheer look of hatred in his eyes. With no clue how to atone for his sins, Frederic placed one hand in his pocket and the other against one of the trees when he arrived.

"Why have you come?" Henry began. "You wish to speak to me?"

Frederic took an immediate step back and looked out at the inky blue waves as they came crashing against the shore. "What can I do?" he asked. "How can I prove my worth?" Desperate to fix things, Frederic glanced over at Henry in a silent plea.

Henry scoffed at the remark and shook his head. "You can't."

Frederic dug his heel into the sand and quirked his mouth to the side.

"I am never going to accept you," Henry confessed. "You have aided the man who has nearly taken everything from me. You stole my sister and brought her here."

"Yes, but I only did those things because—"

Henry held a hand up and silenced him. Then he nodded towards the women he loved as they chatted by the fire. "Do you love her?" His golden gaze drifted from Elaine to Louisa.

Frederic looked at the blonde beauty from afar, hardly able to believe that she loved him. Her presence in his life was like a dream come true, one that he had never dared aspire to. Louisa was good and innocent, sweet and beautiful, precious and kind. While he didn't deserve her, he couldn't deny wanting to please her for the rest of his life.

"Yes," Frederic answered, his eyes on Louisa. "I do. I love her."

Henry pressed his back against the trunk of the tree and adjusted his posture to better suit his injured leg. "Would you mind sitting up later? For the first watch?"

Perking his ears up, Frederic turned back to Henry in relief. "Not at all."

If Frederic could prove to Henry that he only wanted to help, perhaps Henry would move past disagreements of the past. Frederic loved Louisa and wanted to keep her safe. Perhaps pleasing her elder brother would be the only way how.

"Good." Henry pressed his palm into the sand and struggled to stand, gritting his teeth with the pain of forced effort.

"Let me help you." Frederic reached out a hand and clasped Henry's shoulder.

"No!" Henry withdrew immediately and stumbled backward, yet regained his bearings by leaning into the tree. "Please tell my wife that I have lain down to rest."

"Yes, Henry." Frederic lingered nearby. "I will tell her."

Once Frederic watched Henry go, he had no clue whether they had reached an agreement or not. Surely, he would have time to redeem himself, even though he had caused Louisa no harm on the island. If anything, he had been her sole source of protection, saving her life countless times from falling trees, wild beasts and even Judas. But no matter how honorable the rescue may sound, there was no appeasing Henry tonight.

On his trek back to the fire, Frederic hung his head and sighed. How could a demon ever fall in love with an angel? Frederic had worked for the devil, but Louisa had pulled him into the light. Regardless, his troubled past was the only thing Henry was going to go by.

Chapter 7

Elaine slowly breathed in and out, contently nestled in her husband's arms. As she drifted off with her head on his chest, Henry was wide awake, his glowing eyes readily fixed on Frederic's silhouette in the distance. Louisa came running up to Frederic and leapt into his arms, while Henry gritted his teeth and restrained himself from attacking at the sight.

"Lie down with me, Frederic." Louisa took his hands and peered up at him with those sweet blue eyes. "I am ready for bed." She fluttered her lashes and grinned.

Frederic chuckled in the dark, amused at her temperament. "But we have no bed."

Pulling him towards her, Louisa leaned up on the tips of her toes and whispered in his ear. "Then let's make one." She pressed a delicate kiss to his cheek and then ran her fingers through his beard, reveling in the rough, bristly texture.

"Your brother has asked me to stand guard for

the night," he revealed.

Disliking Henry's orders, Louisa pinned her eyebrows together as the angelic grin fled from her face. "But you must sleep, Frederic. The whole night? That is—"

"Your brother has been shot, Louisa." He brushed his thumb along the side of her face. "Time will tell if Elaine has dressed the wound properly."

Louisa turned her cheek into the palm of his hand and frowned in disappointment.

"Henry deserves a good night's rest," Frederic murmured, half regretting his decision to leave Louisa to sleep alone when he had been her constant comfort.

"So do you." Louisa stepped close enough to wrap her arm around his waist.

But Frederic darted his eyes up at the sight of Henry watching them in the distance. Even from afar, he caught the brutal warning piercing the edge of Henry's aura.

"Why don't you join your brother and Elaine?" Frederic withdrew his hand from Louisa's cheek and forced a sliver of space between them. "So you won't be cold."

Absorbing the bitter sting of rejection, Louisa uncoiled her arm from his body and scanned his face with careful concern. "If that is what you wish," she whispered.

"It is." Frederic stared into her bright blue eyes. "Go on now."

Confused and hurt, Louisa stepped backwards in the sand. "Good night, Frederic."

"Good night, dear Louisa." Frederic sank his teeth into his lower lip and balled his hand into a fist at his side the moment she began walking away.

Isolated from the group, Frederic looked on as Louisa approached Henry and Elaine. She hardly said a word to her brother, though Frederic was too far to decipher what. When Louisa lay down on the other side of Elaine, Henry stared at the back of her head for a very long time. By the time she drifted off, he could not contain his silence any longer.

Leaving Elaine and Louisa to dream, Henry rose to his feet and set his hand along the tree to catch his balance. Then he kept his eyes down and limped across the sand until he reached Frederic several hundred yards away. Astounded at his approach, Frederic lowered his head with a welcome nod and swallowed.

"Have you spotted anyone yet?" Henry asked.

"No. Not yet. We should be safe for the night," Frederic predicted.

Despite Henry's six foot stature, Frederic stood nearly three to four inches taller than him. So Henry lifted his head to gaze up at the man who could have killed him with his bare hands if he so desired. "If you love Louisa, you must want what is best for her."

"Why yes," Frederic agreed, searching Henry's

face. "Of course."

"Now that Elaine and I are here, Louisa will be safe again."

"She was safe before," Frederic reasoned. "I kept her safe. I keep her safe."

The corner of Henry's mouth lifted into a patronizing smile. "She was safe before you kidnapped her," he stated. "She would have been safe if you had left her alone in New York. My wife lived on this island as a child, and I have lived here with her."

Frederic closed his mouth and nodded to show that he was listening.

"We can survive. We can protect Louisa. Without you."

Frederic cocked his head to the side as warmth flowed through his body. Reality set in, for Frederic inherently understood the meaning of Henry's words.

"You want me to leave?" Frederic posed. "Abandon Louisa?"

Henry lifted a finger in disagreement. "You won't be abandoning her. Elaine and I are perfectly capable of taking care of Louisa on our own. To be frank, I just don't trust you."

Frederic placed his hands on his hips. "I understand how you feel. Truly, I do but—"

"You are no good for her, Frederic," Henry bluntly stated. "Our father is dead, and I am the man in her life now. I do not approve of the relationship. You will stay away from her."

Surging with disappointment, Frederic scratched his chin and looked over at the distant stretch of sand where Louisa slept. "You plan to keep us apart," he said.

"If our father were alive, he would do the same for her." Henry followed Frederic's line of sight and patted him on the shoulder. "You must know in your heart that it would never work between the two of you. She is still a child, and you are older than I am."

"But Henry, I know you would be better off if I were here." Frederic motioned towards the ground and stared at the cloth tightly wrapped around Henry's leg. "You have been shot. You are wounded. And you know Judas is still lurking in the forest."

"Precisely," Henry noted. "How do I know you aren't spying on all of us on his behalf right now? You've followed his orders before. I've seen you do it."

Frederic stole a glance of sleeping Louisa in the dark and looked out at the sea.

"Stay the night," Henry requested. "But I want you gone by morning."

When Henry turned on his heel to leave, Frederic grabbed his arm. "But Henry. Please," he begged, furrowing his brow in suffering. "I love her."

Henry took a deep breath and shifted to face Frederic. "Then you will let her go."

Utterly lifeless, Frederic stood stock still as

Henry left him alone and made his way back to Elaine and Louisa. After Henry took a seat in the sand and Elaine placed her head in his lap, Frederic peered across the distance at Louisa asleep on the ground. He mashed his lips together and winced, fighting the urge to walk over and convince her to run away with him into the woods. Surely, she would say yes. But he couldn't bring himself to do it.

So Frederic took a step back as thriving hot tears stung his eyes. With one long stride after the next, he walked across the sand and approached the shoreline. Then he sat down in the wet mud and let the waves crash over him, mournfully gazing up at the moon.